What are you

Her gaze shifted t
order counter and
woman taking his order was giving him lots of big
smiles while twirling a strand of her hair. Even at
this distance, it was obvious she was flirting.

Charlotte could see the appeal. John was a strong,
attractive man with a no-nonsense vibe that could
make a girl feel a bit invincible by his side.

Was that what she was doing too? Flirting a little
with her attractive, vigilant colleague?

She paused to consider that scenario, then felt a
rush of heat as she realized it was true. She had
one simple rule when it came to romance on
the road, designed to keep her career intact and
her reputation stellar. No. Dating. Coworkers.
As a travel doctor, she needed excellent
recommendations to secure her next assignment.
She couldn't afford loose ends, bad breakups or
misunderstandings in this line of work.

So John could keep that stacked body of his on his
side of the clinic, because romance was not in the
cards.

Dear Reader,

Greetings! I'm thrilled to share my debut novel for the Harlequin Medical Romance line!

John and Charlotte's story was inspired by the real-life doctors and nurses who care for homeless teens. Whether they work in a strip mall clinic, mobile medical unit, or by strapping on a backpack and working on foot, I knew these doctors deserved their own love story!

Welcome to the Sunshine Clinic, where John heals the homeless teens of Seattle. Gaining guardianship of his spirited niece has forced John to hire Charlotte, a beautiful locum tenens pediatrician, until his life settles down.

Charlotte is equally resentful at being stuck in Seattle to settle her absentee father's estate. Life has taught her to trust adventure over love, so she's fighting her attraction to the brooding, sexy doc with everything she's got.

They're both deeply committed to living life on their terms. If it weren't for an accident that forces Charlotte to share her home with John and his niece, maybe they would have escaped love's healing touch.

Then again, when two people are meant to be together, love always finds a way.

I hope you enjoy John and Charlotte's journey to happily-ever-after!

Love,

Kate

RESISTING THE OFF-LIMITS PEDIATRICIAN

KATE MacGuire

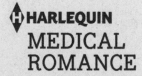

HARLEQUIN
MEDICAL
ROMANCE

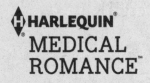

HARLEQUIN®
MEDICAL
ROMANCE™

Recycling programs
for this product may
not exist in your area.

ISBN-13: 978-1-335-59533-1

Resisting the Off-Limits Pediatrician

Copyright © 2024 by Kate MacGuire

For questions and comments about the quality of this book, please contact us at CustomerService@Harlequin.com.

Harlequin Enterprises ULC
22 Adelaide St. West, 41st Floor
Toronto, Ontario M5H 4E3, Canada
www.Harlequin.com

Printed in U.S.A.

Kate MacGuire has loved writing since forever, which led to a career in journalism and public relations. Her short fiction won the Swarthout Award and placed third in the 2020 Women's National Book Association writing contest. Medical romance has always been her guilty pleasure, so she is thrilled to publish her first novel with Harlequin's Medical Romance line. When she's not pounding away on the keyboard, Kate coruns Camp Runamuk with her husband, keeping its two unruly campers in line in the beautiful woodlands of North Carolina. Visit katemacguire.com for updates and stories.

Resisting the Off-Limits Pediatrician

is Kate MacGuire's debut title for Harlequin.

Visit the Author Profile page at Harlequin.com.

This book (and my heart) is dedicated to Patrick.
Thank you for believing in me. Love you…Always.

CHAPTER ONE

SANDY WHITE BEACHES as far as the eye could see… Early-morning sea-kayaking adventures… An elegant evening at the world-class opera house.

Charlotte thumbed through the images on her social media feed. She knew her friends meant well, but every photo of their amazing vacation in Sydney, Australia, was like an icepick to her heart.

Thunder cracked overhead as she waited in line for her rental car. No sandy white beaches here, thank you very much. Instead, she was stuck in her former hometown of Seattle, Washington, right in the middle of one of its legendary rainstorms. She took one last longing glance at her missed vacation before closing her social media feed. That was enough torture for one day.

Every few years she and her friends—all traveling doctors like her—planned an amazing trip to take a break from their locum tenens medical assignments. For their first trip they'd gone to Bora Bora. Then came Madrid, Rome, and

Singapore. These trips, along with her doctor assignments, were captured in her travel blog, *GypsyMD*. She had a small but loyal group of followers who loved her work-hard-play-hard lifestyle as a locum tenens physician.

But the Sydney trip had been the hardest to plan. More of her friends were finding partners, getting married, and settling down with full-time permanent jobs. None of which interested Charlotte, but it sure did make it harder to get enough people interested to justify the expense of the Sydney trip.

Just when she'd solved that problem, her life had taken an unwelcome detour. From out of the blue, a man claiming to be her father's estate attorney had called her.

"It's important that you come to Seattle," he'd said. *"There are some matters related to your father's estate that must be settled."*

Your father.

Two words that sounded so foreign to a girl who'd grown up without one. Once upon a time, when she was much younger, she had daydreamed about her missing father. Was he a rock star who spent every night in a different city? Or maybe a navy captain, steadfastly determined to protect her country's borders? Or a reclusive mountaineer who climbed the world's most treacherous peaks and slept in a yurt?

But in her favorite little-girl dream he was a powerful but despondent king, who used every resource at his disposal to find her. No one would rest, he'd bellow, until his precious, long-lost daughter was returned to her family, safe and sound.

Eventually she'd outgrown those silly day-dreams and accepted her fate. Her father had no idea she existed. So when her mother was killed in a terrible car accident, Charlotte had found herself orphaned at thirteen, with no one to claim her and nowhere to go.

"Ma'am?"

A voice behind her shook Charlotte from her reverie. She mumbled an apology and moved forward with the line. Another crack of thunder overhead released a torrent of rain that fell in sheets against the windows of the airport rental car office. This unexpected trip home was get-ting better by the minute.

An hour later, Charlotte had finished an over-sized coffee and made her way to the address the estate attorney had texted her. The rain had let up a bit, and she paused to gather her thoughts before meeting him. Her view of the house was partially obscured by the steep sloped front yard and its landscaped features of rocks and vegeta-tion, all there to protect against the soil erosion and landslides that came with living in one of

Seattle's hilly neighborhoods. The house appeared to be a two-story split-level, with a large fir tree dominating the front yard.

Someone rapped hard on the passenger window, startling her. A small man with a hooked nose and small, beady eyes peered through the window. "Charlotte? Dr. Charlotte Owens?"

She nodded.

"I'm Jeffrey Bain, your father's attorney."

She nodded, still taking in the home and its upscale neighborhood. She remembered this neighborhood from her childhood. Located northwest of downtown Seattle, the Queen Anne neighborhood was built on a hill with amazing views of the Puget Sound, an inlet of the Pacific Ocean. It was an enclave for Seattle residents who were far more affluent than she and her single mother had been. Once, on a dare, she and a few other teens in her foster care group home had tried trick-or-treating here, to see if they really gave out full-sized chocolate bars, as was rumored. Only one house had.

"Shall we?"

The attorney indicated the house with a short wave of his hand. He seemed to be in just as much of a hurry to get these estate matters settled as she was.

She followed the attorney, navigating the stone steps that climbed the hilly front yard. "You have a beautiful home," she said, noting the professionally designed garden beds and hand-painted ceramic pots along the walkway, though many of the flowers and plants seemed to be languishing.

The attorney gave her a strange glance over his shoulder. "No, ma'am," he said. "*You* have a beautiful home."

Charlotte stopped in her tracks as her brain scrambled to make sense of his words. She had assumed this was the attorney's home, because it didn't make any sense that her father would live here.

"He was just a silly summer fling," her mother had said, when she could be enticed to say anything at all about Charlotte's father. *"He was never going to amount to much."*

All the questions she'd had as a child about her father were swirling in her mind like nosy summer gnats. The attorney unlocked the door and beckoned her inside where the possibility of explanation waited.

She followed him for a breakneck tour of the five-bedroom home. Architecturally speaking, the house was perfect in form and function, design and style. But the wood floors were dull and the windows were dirty. Dust lined the windowsills and spider webs wafted in the corners when she and the attorney passed. Despite touring both floors, she found nothing that explained what her father had become after his summer fling with her mother. There was no evidence of a family. No tick marks on the wall marking a child's growth, no holes in the wall where a teen would have hung posters. Instead, the air was stagnant and sour. Like no one had ever lived here other than ghosts and dust motes.

The tour ended in the kitchen, where the attorney hoisted his oversize briefcase onto the perfect marble countertop, displacing a small cloud of dust. He combed rifled through the files in his briefcase until he found a gray and white folder marked with the emblem of his law firm.

"This is your father's last will and testament, along with his living trust and other important legal documents for your records. Now, as you may be aware, your father lost a great deal of his wealth due to a series of business failures over the last decade of his life. I'm afraid this home is his only real asset, and he has specifically left it to you."

No, she was not aware of any of this. And how could he leave his home to her when he didn't know she existed?

She was about to ask that very question as she thumbed through the legal documents—there were so many! But one caught her attention: *Form JU 04.0100 Petition for Termination of Parent-Child Relationship.*

Charlotte's breath went shallow as she withdrew the document and read it slowly. She was a pediatrician, not a lawyer, but if she understood this right her father had signed an agreement with the state of Washington to forfeit his parental rights. Time slowed as she searched the document for his signature.

It was dated six months after her mother had died.

She continued staring at the document, but the words were blurred, and a horrible rushing sound filled her ears as if a massive runaway train was bearing down on her. Had he known about her all along? Or not until Child Welfare Services had contacted him, informing him that he had a daughter? Either way, he'd known she was orphaned when he'd signed his rights away.

She set the pages down and stepped away from the counter, her chest so tight it burned.

So, her daydreams hadn't been so far-fetched after all. She *was* the long-lost princess daughter of a quasi-king. But knights had never been dispatched to search for her because the King had never yearned for her return.

Inconvenient. Unwanted. Go away.

Anguish uncoiled from deep in her core, its tendrils finding every painful memory of her foster care years that she wanted to forget. How she'd grown up always feeling like an outsider, unwanted and unwelcome. The social workers who'd shown up without warning, giving her a donated suitcase and ten minutes to pack for her next placement. Knowing she would never, ever, find a home of her own. Because everyone knew that families wanted babies, not teenagers.

She squeezed her eyes shut and wished it was ten minutes ago, when she'd thought her painful past was a casualty of fate.

But the petition said otherwise. It said that her father had signed away his rights knowing full well that she would slip into foster care. Shock and hurt quickly gave way to anger. A deep, red-hot rage that demanded to know one thing.

Who does this to a child?

Especially when he'd clearly had the means to care for her.

As if on cue, Charlotte heard the hiss of air brakes. Through the large picture window in the living room that looked out to the street and the Puget Sound beyond, she could see a bright yellow school bus stop in front of the house. Its doors whooshed open and a half dozen kids spilled out, wearing raincoats and rubber boots, whooping with joy as their backpacks bounced with every step that took them back to waiting parents and warm, dry homes.

That could have been her.

That could have been her!

"Why?" she choked out, not trusting her voice to form full sentences.

Why would her father not claim her?

Was there something wrong with her?

She didn't realize she'd spoken the words out loud until the attorney gently slid the folder from her grasp and thumbed through the documents.

"Here," he said, pressing something into her hands.

An envelope, its ivory paper thick and expensive. *Dr. Charlotte Owens* printed on the front.

"Maybe this will explain things," he said, his tone gentle and sympathetic for the first time since they'd met.

Charlotte stared blankly at the letter, as if she had forgotten what envelopes were for. She felt utterly uncertain about what to do next. She considered the contents of the envelope. Good grief, was this her father's attempt to explain himself? To make things right? How dare he? He'd had years to write, call or find her. To do something. To do *anything*! And now he was going to put this on her? Just leave her a letter so he got to have his say while she had none?

The very thought repulsed her so much, it felt like she was holding a snake. She pushed the letter aside so vehemently it would have slid off the counter had Jeffery not caught it first.

"Sell it." Her voice was flat, but steely, her hands curled into fists.

Jeffrey looked at the letter. "Sorry?"

"The house," she clarified. "Just sell it and donate the money to charity."

She wanted nothing to do with anything her father had touched. Why had he even bothered to leave her this house? Was it some kind of torture to make sure she understood all that she had been denied?

She checked her watch and gathered her things. This trip had been a waste of her time. But it wasn't too late to salvage her vacation. If she was lucky, she might catch a late flight to San Francisco, so she could start the long trip to Sydney the next day. With any luck she'd be able to join her friends by the weekend. She could really use some time on a beach chair with a fruity drink before she started her next assignment as ship physician aboard *The Eden*, a massive cruise ship that traveled the Caribbean.

"Wait," Jeffrey said, combing through his briefcase. He fanned a stack of documents before her. Home inspection reports, market analyses, and other incomprehensible paperwork that seemed irrelevant to Charlotte. Until he explained that, despite its desirable zip code and near-perfect facade, the home had been neglected for quite some time. It needed a new roof, there was pervasive mold in the basement, and some structures on the property, like the greenhouse and the pool house, had fallen into such disrepair it was considered hazardous for anyone to enter.

"I'm sorry, but I don't see what this has to do with me." Charlotte shook out her coat, preparing to leave.

The lawyer tidied the pages into a neat stack before clipping them together. "To be blunt, you can't sell the home. I mean, you can try, but no insurance company will cover a house with these problems. And without homeowner's insurance no bank will issue a loan. So, unless you have a cash buyer, this house can't be sold."

Charlotte frowned, her mind racing. "So, are you saying I'm stuck with his house?"

The attorney flicked some invisible lint from his jacket. "Not necessarily. You could sell the property 'as is' to a real estate investment firm. You'll only get a fraction of the home's market value, but you'd be free and clear in a few weeks. In fact…" he rummaged through his seemingly bottomless briefcase "…our firm has an investment division that would be happy to take this property off your hands."

He pushed yet another document her way.

Charlotte's heart leapt at the chance to escape. Just one signature and she could join her friends in Sydney, where the steady tempo of the surf would chase her stress away. Warm sun, cold rum, and friendly locals would help her forget everything that had happened here.

But when she saw the offer amount her pen froze mid-air. She knew a steal when she saw one. Even in its current condition, this house was easily worth three or four times what the firm was offering.

So what? You're going to donate the money to charity. Why do you care?

Maybe that was why she balked. Because this money could do some real good. Charlotte didn't know much about her father, but if he could live in a house like this and not claim his daughter she doubted he had supported many charities. Selling his home and donating the money might be the first good he'd ever done in his life.

It would be wrong to let this attorney lowball her out of the home's true worth. Jeffrey's financial gain wouldn't benefit anyone other than opportunistic investors.

But giving up her travel plans to oversee the renovations felt like a handful of salt in a wound that had never healed. When she'd turned eighteen and aged out of foster care she had vowed that *never* again would others decide her fate. No more social workers and no more donated suitcases. Now she went where she wanted, for as long as she wanted, and stayed only as long as it felt right. That was the beauty of being a traveling doctor. No long-term commitments and she was in total control of her fate.

But what if she had a reason to stay in Seattle beyond renovating her father's home? A purpose that would allow her to leave Seattle with some sense of closure for the harm her father had done? What if she spent *his* money and *her* time helping kids who were in the same situation she'd once been in—alone, vulnerable, scared. Then maybe she would feel justice had been done.

Surely her recruiting agency could help her find a short-term assignment here in Seattle. There had to be a public health clinic or community hospital that could use an extra pediatrician for a few months. If not, she would just volunteer.

Either way, she'd be able to board *The Eden* with a sense of pride. She didn't need her father's wealth, but she could make damn sure that his money would benefit teens who needed it.

She pushed the contract back to the attorney. "Thank you for the offer, Jeffrey. But I have other plans."

The Sunshine Clinic for Kids was a humble brick building that claimed the corner of Fifth and Monroe. Charlotte's heels clicked against the aging sidewalk where stubborn weeds managed to grow in the cracks formed by years of Seattle's rain and low-grade earthquakes. This part of the city was old and industrial, with little concern for aesthetics.

But Charlotte wasn't focused on the factories or the weeds. She was more interested in the clinic itself. The stout little building didn't have the same left behind feel of its neighborhood. Its glass door was polished and flanked by two blue ceramic pots that were spilling over with lush verbena flowers. Lace curtains softened the windows, and in a burst of creativity someone had drawn a bright yellow sun above the clinic's name. There was a relentlessly optimistic feel about the place that appealed to Charlotte. As if the clinic refused to be dragged down by its shabby surroundings.

"Good for you," Charlotte said out loud.

She didn't normally talk to inanimate buildings, but the past few days of being stuck in her father's house was making her a little crazy. Every minute there was a reminder of her father's utter disregard for her well-being when she was still a child.

But finally, she could put all that behind her. The recruiting agency had been thrilled to place her with The Sunshine Clinic, a satellite clinic of Seattle's main hospital, dedicated to providing care for the city's at-risk and homeless teens. She didn't know why her recruiter had been having a hard time finding an interim pediatrician for the clinic, but she was more than ready to lose herself in the demands of a busy day seeing patients. Work and travel had always been her escape from stress and painful emotions. That was how she had sailed through high school with top grades and landed full scholarships to college.

Today was special, so she had chosen her favorite dress. It was light blue, fell just below her knees, and had been handmade by an artist in Sedona, Arizona, where Charlotte had worked at a pediatrics clinic for one summer. When she hadn't been treating the tourists' kids for sunburn and dehydration, she'd used her free time to hike and explore the legendary red rocks of a mountain town reputed to be home to four powerful energy vortexes. Wearing this dress felt like a promise that as soon as the house was ready to sell she'd be back to living life on her terms again.

She struggled to open the clinic door, one arm balancing a box of office supplies and framed diplomas.

"Hello!" she called, but the security system chirped at the same time, obscuring her greeting.

A man was hunched over the reception counter, his back to her, with a phone pressed to his ear, oblivious to her presence. She took in his dark jeans and motorcycle boots, along with a leather jacket that strained to contain his broad, muscular shoulders. Was he a patient or an employee of the clinic? She couldn't tell. But the open ladder near the counter made her think he might be something to do with maintenance.

Whoever he was, he was not having a good day.

"But Mrs. Winthrop, at least she used her words, right?" The man forced a chuckle. "No, I agree. It's inappropriate for an eleven-year-old to use *those* words." After a few *mm-hmms* and *yes, I sees*, he suddenly straightened. "Oh, no, that won't be necessary." There was a silence as he pressed the phone harder to his ear. "Well… yes, but you see…" His shoulders slumped in defeat. "Mrs. Winthrop, please. I'm begging you. This is Piper's third school this year…" There was a long pause before he suddenly brightened. "Oh, thank you! I appreciate that." He ran his thumb along the edge of the counter, smoothing an imperfection that was invisible to Charlotte. "I promise that we *will* be working on this at home."

His leather jacket shifted when he hung up the phone, revealing the V-shape of his back and waist. Charlotte bit her lip as she watched him pinch the bridge of his nose. It was obvious she had overheard a private phone call. She hated to intrude on his apparent distress, but today was her first day and she didn't want to be late. She needed to report to Dr. John Bennett, the clinic's director, as soon as possible.

She cleared her throat. "Hello?"

The man spun to face her. For several long seconds Charlotte felt a kind of shock to her system that momentarily stole her words and purpose. The strength she had seen his leather jacket struggling to contain was also found in the thick muscles of his chest and neck. He had a handsome, honest face and wore his chestnut-brown hair long to his collar, the waves still shower-damp. He was rugged and masculine, and maybe a bit intimidating with that intense scowl.

Or maybe it was his eyes that pinned her in place. Greenish gold, like the eyes of coyotes and cougars, his gaze was so intense she felt like a rabbit that had wandered too far into apex predator territory.

She swallowed hard as she noticed the stethoscope around his neck. Though he bore little resemblance to the bland headshot posted on the hospital's website, this was Dr. John Bennett, her new colleague.

For heaven's sake, Charlotte. Stop staring and say something!

But he saved her the trouble. He folded his arms across his impressive chest and assessed her with a measured stare. "Dr. Owens, right? The locum doctor?"

Charlotte wiggled the lapel of her lab coat where her name was embroidered in black thread. "Guilty as charged!" she said, hating her too-cheerful tone.

The first day of a new job was the worst. She loved the freedom that came with being a traveling doctor, but being "the new doc" took its toll.

"Paperwork, please," he said, finally shifting his focus from her to rummage through his toolbox. "So we can get you on your way." He found whatever he was looking for and started to climb the ladder.

"Paperwork?"

"You know… Whatever the courts gave you to track your community service so you can get your medical license reinstated. I'll sign off to say that you're making a good faith effort to find a service site and you can be on your way."

Charlotte had felt off-kilter ever since she'd walked through the door. This conversation was not helping. "I'm sorry, I don't know what you're talking about."

He paused, a screwdriver gripped between his teeth. He removed it to ask, "Then why are you here?"

Charlotte was starting to wonder if Gina, her recruiter, had made a mistake with this assignment. Only that would explain this surreal conversation.

"Because you need a locum pediatrician. At least that's what I was told."

Her new colleague chuckled and shook his head. "Depends on who you ask, I suppose."

As if that should satisfy her curiosity, he tucked the screwdriver in his back pocket and climbed back up the ladder.

What did that mean? And what was she supposed to do next? The box she was holding was growing heavier by the minute. She'd like to set it down on the counter, but the strange man was occupying that space, so she chose one of the orange vinyl chairs near the picture window instead. Then she found her phone and contemplated calling Gina, to make sure she was in the right place. But she'd worked with Gina for years, long enough to know that Gina double-checked every detail before sending one of her doctors to a new assignment. There was no way she was in the wrong place or had the wrong information.

Whatever was wrong here, her new colleague seemed to be at the heart of it.

John Bennett started whistling a tune—something familiar, but she couldn't quite place the melody. And she didn't care because she was getting annoyed. For Pete's sake, she was standing right here. Why was he refusing to talk to her or deal with her?

Before she knew exactly what she was going

to do, she strode over and gave the ladder a tiny shake. "Hey!"

"Hey!" he yelled back. "Do you mind?"

"Actually, I do. Do I have a job here or not?"

She braced herself for a fight, but from this angle, looking up at him, she could see a slight crook in his nose, hinting that he was no stranger to fights much worse than what she was bringing.

He leaned one arm on the ladder and studied her like she was a specimen under a microscope. "Well, that depends. Because so far everyone interested in the job has been a pretty desperate character. Either they need community service hours to get their medical license reinstated or they are serving probation for some kind of legal trouble." He tucked the light fixture back in the ceiling and started tightening screws. "We don't need any of that nonsense around here."

"I'm not a desperate character!" Unless you counted her desperation to get away from her father's house and all of its painful memories.

John paused his tinkering long enough to indicate her entire person with a wave of his screwdriver. "I don't know about desperate, lady. But that dress definitely makes you a character."

A flare of heat bloomed in her cheeks as she realized this John didn't want her in his clinic. Just like her father hadn't wanted her in his life. Which was fine by her. She was sick of being pushed around by the inexplicable whims of men who wielded their power with a reckless disregard for how they hurt others.

She stalked back to the window and grabbed her box of personal belongings. A familiar bravado infused her core. Gina could find her another noble cause to keep her busy while she was stuck in Seattle. Or maybe she should abandon this plan to do some good while she was here. It wasn't too late to follow her first impulse and sell her father's house "as is" and get her derriere over to Sydney.

She was halfway to the door when she spied that shaky yellow sun hovering above the clinic's name. Who had drawn that? Had it been one of the teens who'd passed through here, desperate for something pretty and warm to brighten the world? Or an employee—perhaps the same employee who had planted flowers at the front door and hung lacy curtains in the windows?

Someone was working awfully hard to make this clinic a refuge for the teens who found their way here. It wasn't Dr. Sunshine-on-a-Ladder over there, that was for sure. But someone here had known darkness and loss. And also that the tiniest gesture of hope could pull you through the darkest nights.

Her shoulders slumped as the fight left her. What kind of doctor would she be if she turned her back on vulnerable teens after a little friction with a grumpy doctor? She huffed an exasperated sigh as she set her box back down on the orange vinyl chair.

John was off the ladder now, rummaging through his tools. If he'd noticed her near-exit, he was keeping a pretty good poker face about it.

"So." She crossed her arms. "Where's my office?"

He glanced up, a tiny glimmer of surprise in his eyes before he recovered his stoic expression. Had she had surprised him? If so, good. John looked like he needed someone to rattle his cage once in a while.

He closed his toolbox and latched it shut before turning back to Charlotte, arms folded across his chest. "If you're going to stick around, we have to fix this first." He indicated her entire person with a chin-thrust.

"Pardon me?"

His gaze moved like an elevator from her head to her shoes before he shook his head. "Didn't the agency tell you how to dress?"

Her urge to snipe back was strong, but if they were going to get anything done they needed to have an actual conversation.

"Here, give me that." He proffered his hand, clearly wanting something from her, and she detected a hint of his cologne. Clean, with musky male undernotes and hints of spice and surprise.

"Give you what?"

"Your lab coat." He beckoned with a quick wave of his fingers.

The man made less sense by the minute. Why on earth did he want her lab coat? Still, he was at least speaking to her now, and that seemed like progress.

She shrugged off her coat and handed it over.

"Do you have anything else you could wear? Something less...bohemian?"

That familiar quick flash of anger flared again. "This isn't bohemian. It's practically a work of art. It was hand-stitched in Sedona by a textile artist whose work is in high demand."

But that wasn't why she'd bought it. She just loved the whimsy of a blue dress printed with sycamore trees, pink owls tucked in their branches.

"Is that so? Well, you don't see many hand-stitched works of art around here, which means you're going to stick out. Not the effect we're going for, Dr. Owens, so please, follow me."

Curiosity compelled her to follow him down a narrow hallway to a storage closet where he dragged out several boxes labeled *Donations*. Then he dug through the clothing, checking tags and tossing items aside, until he held up a pair of faded green cargo pants. "These might work," he said.

Charlotte hooked a finger through the belt loop. "For what?"

He didn't respond. He was too busy digging through the box until he found a salmon-hued graphic tee shirt. After years of washing, its letters were faded and peeling, but she could still make out *Fort Lauderdale, Florida. Est 1911.*

He pointed to a door behind her. "You can change in there. But I can't help you with the shoes."

Charlotte looked down at her simple flats.

"From now on you need to wear closed-toe athletic shoes."

Her head was spinning. What was happening here?

He grabbed a box of baby wipes from the shelf. "The lipstick—it's got to go. And the earrings. And the bangles." He paused and assessed her with a critical eye. "And your hair." He indicated her long, dark hair, which she wore in loose waves past her shoulders. "Just try to draw less attention to yourself. Be like a lamppost— there, but not really seen. Okay?"

"You want me to look like a lamppost?"

He shook his head, exasperated. "No, I don't want you to look like a lamppost. Just be less... striking, okay?" He groaned as if he hadn't meant to say that, running a rough hand through his hair.

Charlotte caught a glimpse of herself in the hallway mirror, crumpled clothes and baby wipes in her hand. "Dr. Bennett, this seems very unprofessional."

His green eyes softened for the first time since they'd met. "Good. Then maybe the kids will talk to you. Tell you where it hurts."

He headed back to the waiting room, leaving Charlotte alone. She went into the small bathroom and tried to recover her equilibrium. It wasn't like she'd expected a parade just for showing up. But she sure hadn't expected to be butting heads with her new colleague on day one.

She puffed an errant strand of hair away from her eyes. "So much for saving the world," she said to her reflection.

Was this why Gina had had such trouble filling this position? Who knew how many well-meaning doctors had been here before her, wanting to help, only to get run off by a good-looking but grumpy doctor?

She slipped off her dress, trading it for the tee shirt and cargo pants. John had guessed her size just right. She liked the shirt, soft and cozy after years of washing, but it was hard to shake off the unwanted flashback to her younger self, when she'd had to take whatever hand-me-downs were given to her.

"So go," she whispered to her image. "You don't have to stay…"

Easy-breezy was her life's motto. *Travel light and keep things casual and fun.*

That was how she'd stayed one step ahead of the heartbreak and loss that had stained her teen years. But Dr. Bennett looked like he was anything but easy-breezy.

Conflicting thoughts swirled in her head. This assignment was going to be tough, for sure. But life was full of tough challenges. That was what it took to reveal true character. And if she missed this opportunity to make a difference in the lives of teens who needed her, then she'd be a lot more like her father than she wanted to admit.

She took a deep breath to steady herself, then started arranging her hair into a French braid.

She wasn't going anywhere—whether John liked it or not.

CHAPTER TWO

JOHN CLIMBED BACK up the ladder to finish his repairs. He didn't have time for these extra tasks, but filing a work order with the hospital's maintenance department meant waiting weeks for someone to show. Out here, deep in Seattle's industrial district, his little satellite clinic wasn't a big priority for the administrative types.

Which was fine by him. If being the king of his clinic meant doing the maintenance, so be it. It kept the top brass from breathing down his neck and let him do things his way. The same way he'd been doing things since his father had walked out on his family, leaving John charged with keeping his little brother Michael out of trouble while their mom worked two or three jobs to keep their heads above water. Not an easy task for John—especially with Michael's iron will and mad Houdini-esque escape artist skills.

But Michael wouldn't be escaping anytime soon. He'd been sentenced to five years in prison on drug charges, making John the legal guardian of Piper, his eleven-year-old niece. But, despite his best efforts, Piper was not settling into her new life with her bachelor uncle on his live-aboard sailboat very well. She was frequently in trouble at school, which meant now the hospital was breathing down John's neck plenty, on account of his many missed shifts so he could meet with Piper's principal or fill in when an exasperated sitter quit on the spot.

Those missed shifts had eventually caught the attention of the chief of pediatrics, who'd decreed that adding a locum doctor to the clinic would be better than relying on on-call doctors to fill in. John had done his best to assure the pediatric team that he had everything under control. The last thing he needed was another doctor in his space, messing up the systems that he and Sarah, his receptionist and medical assistant, had spent years perfecting.

And most of the locums who had applied so far had had their own agenda—like documenting community service hours to get a medical license reinstated. He had worked too hard to earn the trust of Seattle's vulnerable teens to let anyone like that through the front door. And the good doctors just didn't stick around. The long hours and limited resources made it too tempting to accept positions with the main hospital or pediatric private practices.

So he probably didn't need to worry about the tall brunette who was now carefully folding her dress. Two weeks—four, tops—and she'd be one more doctor who'd ghosted him for a better opportunity, leaving him alone to take care of everything.

At least she looked better now that she had changed. Not that she'd looked terrible before. She was actually quite stunning, with that Grecian profile and soft blue eyes. But the rumpled tee shirt and casual braid made her more approachable, which the teens needed. Many had trust issues with adults, so he had learned to ditch anything that made him look like an authority figure.

She hoisted the box and turned to face him. "Where's my office?"

So she was sticking around despite his unsolicited wardrobe consultation. *Interesting.*

"You don't have an office. Sorry." He'd had to sacrifice his own to create a second exam room for the steady parade of locum doctors who had come and gone before her. He folded the ladder and leaned it against the wall. "But I can add some shelving to your exam room if you want."

"Where am I supposed to do my charting? Or phone in scripts and consults?"

He pointed behind the reception desk, where he had set an old door across two sawhorses.

Two computers and a single phone marked the office space.

She narrowed her eyes and he braced himself for another clash. He liked how her blue eyes darkened when she was irritated. A man could learn to read a woman like that, he thought, the same way a sailor could read the skies for signs of trouble.

But Sarah saved him from the impending squall by breezing into the clinic. She hustled behind the front desk, organizing her coat and purse before she noticed Charlotte.

"Oh, honey!" she exclaimed. "You must be the new doctor!" She set Charlotte's box on the counter so she could pull her into one of the famous Mother Bear hugs the teens loved. Then she stepped back, her hands cupping Charlotte's shoulders. "Ready for some coffee and a tour?"

Now, why hadn't he thought of that? Coffee and a tour would have been a far more civilized way to start the day.

John half listened as Sarah led Charlotte on a tour of the real-estate-office-turned-medical-clinic. They had maximized their small space by using office partitions and creative design to create two exam rooms, an onsite pharmacy and lab, and a food pantry where kids could grab snacks and drinks to go. It was half as much as John had wanted when he'd started the clinic five years ago but, as Sarah often reminded him, Rome wasn't built in a day.

"And here we are, back where we started," Sarah said, her hands set low on her hips.

Charlotte rounded the corner and he caught her eyes for a moment. Everything about her—from her resume, which read like a travel brochure, to her sun-kissed smooth skin—hinted at freedom, wanderlust, adventure. She was like a telegraph from his Before Times, when he had been free to spend his time as he liked. Mostly that had translated to long hours at the clinic, then spending his free time rehabbing *The House Call*, the sailboat he called home, to prepare for his next trip into the open waters beyond the Puget Sound. It was a little too easy to imagine Charlotte's long, lithe body at the helm of *The House Call*, the wind whipping her dark hair and her eyes wild with delight.

But there would be no voyages now—nor wild-eyed women on his boat or in his bed. Not with Piper as his charge. The mistakes he had made with his brother had robbed Michael of his freedom and his future. Mistakes he would not repeat—which was why it didn't matter that Charlotte smelled like jasmine and rain. He'd be sticking to his side of the clinic until the trade winds that had blown her into Seattle blew her somewhere else.

By noon, the clinic was in chaos. The waiting room was standing room only, with teens laughing and buzzing like a swarm of cicadas. A tower of mail and magazines threatened to spill off the reception counter. Sarah was running triage, somehow taking calls and screening walkins without losing her mind.

John walked his last patient to Sarah for checkout just as Charlotte left her office. She had Matthew with her, a quiet boy John knew from his previous visits. Something about Matthew's uneasy expression and the stack of prescription slips in his hand tripped John's radar.

"For starters," Charlotte said, "you'll need to avoid triggers like smoke, pollen, and cold weather."

John willed himself to stay on his side of the clinic, as he had vowed. He didn't need to get in the middle of every single thing that happened.

Matthew squinted at one of the slips. "What's a nebulizer?"

Okay, maybe he did. Cripes, she'd prescribed a *nebulizer*? Didn't she know some of these kids didn't have…?

No, of course she didn't. This wasn't her world—it was his. And whether he wanted a partner or not, he had one now. It was up to him to make sure she understood what she had signed up for.

He joined them at the reception counter. "May I see those?" he asked, indicating the prescriptions. He thumbed through them one by one. "Advair disks...excellent choice." He crumpled the slip and stuck it in his pocket. "If state insurance covered them."

Charlotte's brow furrowed.

He looked at the next slip. "Steroids—good. Let's add an antihistamine and a generic bronchodilator. Sarah can find those in our pharmacy." Which wasn't a pharmacy at all, but a storage closet stocked with the medications they prescribed most often. "Now, let's talk about your digs."

Sarah swiveled in her chair, a phone receiver pressed to her ear. "I've got the House of Hope on the line. He's got a bed."

"And a caseworker?"

"Working on it!" She patted the chair next to her, indicating Matthew should sit with her while she worked.

Suddenly Charlotte's hand was on John's arm, squeezing hard. "How am I supposed to help these kids if I can't give them what they need? You know as well as I do that Matthew needs more than steroids and allergy meds!"

The intensity of her expression matched the pressure of her grip. Was she a Type A person, then, intent on excelling at whatever she tried?

Or did she actually care if Matthew got the help he needed?

John sighed and slid his pen behind his ear. "You prescribed a nebulizer, right? Which requires electricity?"

"Of course."

"So, does Matthew have consistent access to electricity?"

She frowned. "I don't know."

"And the Advair disks? Insurance doesn't cover the branded version, so he'll need the generic—which we don't stock. So where is the closest pharmacy? What bus routes does Matthew need to get there?"

Her grip on his arm loosened. "I don't know that either."

He reached behind the counter, then slid a bus route planner in front of her. "Well, study up, Doc. Because this is part of your job too."

She looked up at him, her hand still draped on his arm, her eyes shiny—with anger or distress? He couldn't tell. "Why is he even on the street? Why not in a shelter or a foster home—someplace safe?"

Because life was inherently unfair. End of story. There was no point dwelling on *who* or *why* or *should* and *could*. All that mattered was being there for the teens who needed them and doing what they could for as long as they could.

"Kids like Matthew have it tough. There are only a few shelters in Seattle that are certified to accept unaccompanied minors, and they have long waiting lists. That's why they need meds they can stuff in their pockets or shoes. It's not ideal—I know that. But if we can help, they'll start to trust us. That's when we can make a difference."

Charlotte stepped away, her gaze avoiding his as her fingers fidgeted with a loose thread on the hem of her shirt. Her forehead puckered, as if she was working something out. He'd seen that look before, in the doctors who had come before her. He braced himself for The Talk, full of reassurances that *It's not you, it's not the kids...it's me.*

But she surprised him.

"You know what we should do? We should set up an area where kids could come by for breathing treatments when we're open." She was stalking the clinic now, looking through doorways and assessing every room.

John felt like a puppy as he trailed her. "I'm sorry...what? We don't have the budget or the space for..."

"And we should stock more brand-name drugs. Pharmaceutical companies donate drugs all the time. I'm sure there's a process—and lots of forms, of course. But we can figure it out!"

We? When had they become a "we"?

John cleared his throat. "I appreciate your enthusiasm, Dr. Owens. But we don't have the space to add a breathing treatment area. And Sarah doesn't have the time to set up and monitor a drug donation partnership."

"Just Charlotte is fine. It won't be difficult, I promise. If we move a partition here or there we can make the space. Then we could contact the university and become a practicum site for nursing students. They could oversee the breathing treatment area in exchange for getting firsthand experience in community medicine."

She was bold—he had to give her that. Bold and provocative and a little sexy, with those intense and determined blue eyes.

"These are very ambitious ideas, Dr. Owens, and I appreciate—"

"Charlotte," she corrected him again.

"Charlotte, I appreciate your enthusiasm—I do. But we have our hands full providing the services we already have."

Not that he didn't want to offer the teens more. When he'd started he'd been full of ambitious plans to grow the tiny storefront clinic into a full-service medical, dental, and behavioral health clinic, able to provide all the care Seattle's vulnerable teens deserved.

But there was only so much that he and Sarah could do on their own. And, while Sarah had been nagging him to start thinking about how he would replace her when she finally retired for good, he could not imagine entrusting the clinic and its teen patients to anyone other than himself and Sarah.

"I couldn't possibly ask Sarah to take on more—"

Charlotte flashed him an absolutely brilliant smile. "Sarah doesn't have to do a thing. You have me now! I'll start researching the medication program tonight."

Then she powered up her computer tablet and scanned the day's appointments as if she'd worked there all her life.

John stood for a moment, hands fisted at his sides, thoroughly annoyed at the flare of attraction that bloomed in his chest. Everything she'd suggested was exactly how he wanted to grow the clinic. Could it be different if he had a partner? Could someone like Charlotte figure out how to overcome obstacles that had stymied him?

For one long minute it was tempting to lean into the hope he felt stirring in his chest.

But no, he wouldn't do it. It was too risky. The teens and the hospital relied on him to keep the clinic running, day after day. The last thing he needed was to build something with Charlotte, only to have her take off when wanderlust struck, leaving him to pick up the pieces. It was better for him to stick to what he could manage on his own, year after year.

His musings were interrupted when the front door was flung open hard and fast, hitting the wall at the same time as the security alarm chirped twice.

"Hey, Doc!" a girl's frantic voice called. "This kid needs help!"

John knew who it was without looking. Angel was a frequent visitor to The Sunshine Clinic, often dragging along a kid who needed help while refusing any for herself.

Today was no different. She had one arm slung around the shoulders of a freckle-faced boy who wiped his nose on his sleeve, looking more confused than sick.

Sarah peered at the girl over her bifocals. "The door, Angel. We've discussed this, remember?"

"Right!" Angel dashed back and shut the door quietly, her long ponytail swinging wildly with every step. "Sorry."

Sarah oversaw the check-in process for the boy, Bruce, while John contemplated how to handle Charlotte's plans for the clinic. He didn't want to crush her enthusiasm for helping the teens, but he wasn't going to start anything with Charlotte that he couldn't finish.

"Angel, would you please take Bruce to Exam Room Two?" Sarah said.

John's head snapped up. That was Charlotte's exam room.

John willed himself to wait until Angel had led Bruce out of earshot. "Sarah, what are you doing? Angel's case is far too complicated for Charlotte's first day."

"Angel?" Charlotte asked, clearly confused. "I thought Bruce was the patient?"

Sarah explained Angel's habit of bringing other kids to the clinic. "But we're worried about Angel."

"Or whoever she is," John continued. "We don't know, because she won't tell us her real name. What we do know is that sometimes she presses her chest, as if it hurts. And she's admitted to having a few dizzy spells. She won't consent to an exam, but even if she did I can't treat her until she qualifies for state medical insurance."

Charlotte bit her bottom lip as she listened. "And you can't get her qualified for insurance without a real, legal name, right?"

"Right," Sarah confirmed. "That's why I think you should be the one to see her. You're brand-new here. Maybe there will be something about you that will get her to open up."

"But this is Charlotte's first day!" John protested. "She doesn't know anything about Angel's case. More importantly, Angel doesn't know her. There's no rapport there…no trust."

"I know she trusts you, John, but despite your best efforts you haven't been able to get Angel to consent to a physical exam. If we don't make progress soon, whatever's wrong with her could get a lot worse."

Every cell in John's body was on alert. It had taken him months to build a rapport with Angel, but despite his lectures and gentle cajoling Angel still would not agree to an exam or reveal her name.

Sarah was right. For Angel's sake, he had to give Charlotte a chance to get past Angel's defenses.

He gave a quick nod of agreement. "But be careful, Charlotte. No pushing her, okay? If she wants to talk—" *she wouldn't* "—great. But if not, just back off. Otherwise she'll run away and we may never see her again."

Charlotte nodded and headed down the hall. John followed close behind, feeling jittery with frustration. He knew Sarah was right to see if Charlotte could have a breakthrough with Angel, but it felt like just one more area of his life where he was losing control.

Not that his life before getting guardianship of Piper had been perfect. He'd worked long hours at the clinic and sailed alone on the sea. But it had been *his* life to live the way he saw fit, and he'd liked it just fine.

Now he felt his world churning beneath his feet, as if a fierce storm was headed his way.

Charlotte closed the door behind her and assessed her young patients. Bruce sat on the exam table, relaxed and curious. Angel stood in the corner of the room, her back up against the wall, arms crossed across her chest, her expression suspicious.

"Where's Dr. J?" she demanded.

"Busy with other patients," Charlotte answered truthfully, because the waiting room was about to burst at the seams. "I'm Dr. Charlotte Owens."

Then she cringed, because that sounded so formal. Was it better to introduce herself as Dr. C, borrowing the teen's shortened name for John? That didn't feel right. She realized she had no idea how to get things off to a good start with kids who didn't trust her as readily as the patients she usually treated.

It would be nice to ask John for some guidance, but apparently she didn't know how to get things off to a good start with him either. Was he this unfriendly to all the locums who'd come before her? Or was there something special about her that brought out his snarky side?

"So tell me, Bruce, what brings you in today?"

It wasn't Bruce who answered, though. Angel immediately responded, describing Bruce's sneezing, watery eyes, and occasional cough. She seemed very comfortable in the medical setting. *Interesting*, Charlotte thought. Angel had clearly been mothered by someone who'd taken her to the doctor. So where was that parent now?

"Well, let's take a look, shall we?"

Charlotte soon ruled out any serious infection or a virus. Bruce didn't have a fever and his lymph nodes were just slightly enlarged. Enough to indicate his immune system was on alert, but not fighting anything serious.

"Looks like seasonal allergies, Bruce," Charlotte said, making a note in his file.

"So he'll need antihistamines, then," Angel said, still serious and motherly. That was another surprise, because most teens didn't talk like that.

How old was she anyway? Charlotte did a quick visual.

Angel wore a lot of makeup, had big hoop earrings, and carried herself tall and strong. Late high school was Charlotte's best guess, maybe close to graduation. Charlotte remembered what it had been like to be on the cusp of graduation, on the verge of losing the fragile support she'd had through foster care. It hurt her heart to think that Angel was already fending for herself when she was still in high school.

"That's right, he will. Do you prefer chewable or can you swallow pills?" Charlotte asked Bruce.

"Pills."

She typed up the visit notes along with an order for a month's supply of allergy medication. "Bruce, take this to Sarah. She'll get your medication and get you checked out."

Angel stood to follow him and Charlotte held her breath, hoping for the best. "Hey, Angel, would you mind sticking around for a minute?"

Angel paused, her hand on the doorknob. She gave Charlotte a long, appraising look before she slowly walked back and stood in the corner, recrossing her arms against her chest.

Charlotte slowly exhaled with relief. Finally, she had a chance to make a difference here—which was the whole reason she wanted to work at The Sunshine Clinic.

"What do you want?"

Charlotte took care to keep her distance, positioning herself away from the door so Angel knew she could leave whenever she wanted. But Charlotte hoped she wouldn't.

"I just wanted to talk a little, if that's okay."

"About what?"

"About you, I suppose."

Angel's eyes narrowed. Everything about her, from her tensed body to her focused gaze, spoke of distrust and fear.

"Dr. J told me that your chest hurts sometimes. And you also get dizzy?"

Angel shrugged. "It doesn't happen that often."

"That's good. But you're pretty young for chest pain. How old are you anyway?"

Angel gave her a knowing look and shook her head. "Nice try, Doc."

So Angel was withholding *all* personal information, not just her name. Did she not want to be found? Was it possible she had a head trauma or an illness that affected her memory so that she truly didn't know who she was? Or had she found one small way to seize control of something in a world that had spun hopelessly off its axis?

Charlotte continued. "Angel, there's a lot of reasons why you might have these symptoms, like dehydration, stress or fatigue. But there's also some pretty scary ones. I'd like to do an exam, if that's okay, or at least listen to your heart for a bit."

That only seemed to make Angel double down on her tough girl facade. She jutted her chin forward, more determined than ever. "I'm not scared."

But there was a flicker in her eyes that said otherwise, and she was starting to cast side glances at the door.

Charlotte's stomach fluttered with alarm. How

was she going to help this girl if the mere mention of a medical exam triggered her flight response?

Stay calm and think. Find a way.

Then Charlotte noticed Angel's necklace. She wore a pendant with four interlocked hearts. The first one was solid gold while the others were hollow. A hazy memory from Charlotte's foster home days slowly rose to the surface.

"That's a sister's necklace, right?"

Angel's hand reflexively flew to her neck. "I guess."

"And you're the oldest, right? That's why the first heart is solid?"

"Yeah."

Charlotte's mind sifted through the possibilities for connection. It was clear that Angel's need for control was too strong for her to accept help. Not for herself, anyway.

But maybe for her sisters, she would.

"I'm worried about them, Angel. Your sisters, that is."

Angel's brows furrowed. "Why? You don't even know them."

"True. But I know that many heart conditions are hereditary. So, if you're sick…"

"My sisters could have it too?" Angel's defiant expression melted into worry.

"It's possible. The only way to know for sure is to find out if your heart is healthy."

A great war of emotions played out across the canvas of Angel's face. Charlotte bit her lip, hoping against hope that her love for her sisters was enough to push her beyond her comfort zone.

"Okay, fine." She turned and jumped up on the exam table.

Charlotte quickly completed the exam, limiting herself to what was essential. Angel was thinner than Charlotte would like, and she would have loved to check her blood cell counts and nutritional status. But Charlotte limited herself to focusing on Angel's heart, warming the stethoscope drum before laying it against the girl's thin chest. She took her time, listening from all angles to make sure she was right.

"Thank you, Angel." Charlotte stood and draped her stethoscope around her neck, considering her approach.

"So?" Angel asked, adjusting her shirt. "Am I okay?"

Charlotte smiled. "Overall, you look really healthy, Angel. But your heart is beating faster than it should. We need to figure out why."

"Can't you just give me a pill or something?"

"That might be an option, once we know what's wrong. That's why I need to refer you to a cardiologist for an EKG." Charlotte silently chided herself for the doctor talk. "In other words, I'd like you to see a heart specialist. They'll want to do an

EKG, which is a painless test that gives us more information about how your heart is working."

Angel avoided Charlotte's gaze as she jumped off the table and headed for the door. For one moment, Charlotte feared Angel would just walk out the door and never return.

But Angel paused, her hair falling to block her face. "This would help my sisters?"

Charlotte's heart clutched with compassion. She wanted Angel to know it was important to help herself too. "It would be a good start. But it could lead to more testing to figure out what's really wrong."

For several long seconds, Charlotte stayed perfectly still, waiting to see what Angel would do.

Come on, girl. Take a chance on me. I won't let you down.

"Maybe," Angel whispered, before slipping out the door.

That was not the answer Charlotte wanted to hear. Tachycardia could be caused by a lot of things, some of them quite serious. If Angel had a congenital heart issue, her heart could be a ticking time bomb, just waiting for a day when she exercised too hard or was otherwise stressed to go into full cardiac arrest.

Where did Angel go? When would she come back?

Would she ever get another chance to help her?

Charlotte dropped her head to her hands, overwhelmed with the weight of this work. She'd come here determined to make a difference in the lives of teenagers who had no one looking out for them. But how could she help kids who didn't have a permanent address or phone number? Or a clean place to sleep or safe places to store their medicine?

And could she even help a girl so determined to live like a ghost?

Charlotte made her way back to her makeshift office. John was already there, recording his notes on the computer.

Charlotte dropped into the chair next to him.

"So, how did it go?" he asked.

Charlotte let her head drop back until it rested on the back of her chair. She didn't want to tell him he was right. But he was. "Exactly the way you said it would. Except…" She held up an index finger to mark her point. "I did get her to consent to a basic physical exam."

John's fingers hovered over the keyboard. "And?"

"You were right again. She has significant tachycardia that needs to be checked out by a cardiologist."

John spun in his chair to face her. "And she agreed?"

Damn it. Every cell in her body wanted to say

she had made the connection with Angel that John thought was impossible. For Angel's sake, of course. But also to prove that she belonged there, to John and maybe even to herself.

"No, she didn't," Charlotte conceded. "But she didn't say no either. In fact, I got a 'maybe' before she left the office. Kind of in a hurry."

"Was she freaked out?"

"Not freaked out. Just not happy."

John rubbed the back of his neck and looked off into the distance, as if he might be able to catch a glimpse of Angel before her tiny frame disappeared into the city.

"So what does that mean? Will she come back?"

Judging from his worried body language, John didn't know either. And that was when Charlotte realized she had signed up for something she didn't understand. How was she going to make this grand difference in the universe when she didn't even know who her patients were or when they would come back?

"All we can do is earn her trust over time…on her schedule," John said.

His sigh was heavy as he turned his bulky frame back to the tiny keyboard and resumed his hunt-and-peck technique. He was so earnest as he studied the screen, deliberately typing each word. It was tempting to tease him a little, but she wasn't sure if John was the teasing type. In fact, she knew very little about him.

If she was going to have any chance of making a difference at The Sunshine Clinic, she needed to understand the kids who came here. One person in this place clearly had that gift, and he was currently squinting at the screen with a pencil clasped between his teeth.

"So…" Charlotte said, fiddling with the pocket on her cargo pants. "If—I mean *when* Angel comes back, we should have some sort of plan for her EKG, right? Maybe we could work together on making that happen?"

John looked her way, a flicker of surprise in his eyes. He really was a handsome man when he wasn't scowling. Intelligent green eyes, smooth, olive-toned skin. And a sculpted jaw that would make Michelangelo weep.

Charlotte willed herself to look away, but her gaze lingered on his mouth a beat too long and her cheeks grew warm when he caught her staring.

Sarah paused in typing away on her keyboard and spun her chair to face them.

"Oh, John, you should take her to Guido's for lunch. It's been ages since you've had a real break from the clinic. And I think it would be lovely for you two to get to know each other."

Something in Sarah's tone sounded slightly

provocative, like she was suggesting a date rather than a working lunch between colleagues. Good grief, did John think that was what she was thinking? Because she wasn't! She just wanted to talk about Angel and how to get her to a specialist.

Did he feel put on the spot too?

If so, he didn't seem bothered. If anything, his moss-green eyes seemed a bit softer now as he studied her. Making her feel less like a specimen and more like a…a friend?

"Sure," John agreed affably. "I'd love to get to know my new colleague."

CHAPTER THREE

IT WAS MORE than a week later before they could carve out some time for their lunch date. John kept a tight schedule, often skipping lunch so he could fit in one more appointment or spend extra time with a teen who had complex medical needs.

By the time they set out on the short, four-block walk to Guido's Mexican Cantina, Charlotte had been thinking about their lunch for days. John's plan to earn Angel's trust over time wasn't sitting right with her. Not with Angel's fast heartbeat and dizzy spells. They needed to be ready to help her as soon as she returned, whether she shared her real name with them or not.

Despite it being early, the cantina was crowded when they arrived. With its ombre orange walls and wrought-iron decor, the café felt like a Spanish Gothic man cave. On the back wall, near the kitchen, a stenciled jet-black bull posed, its nostrils flared, with one menacing hoof poised to stamp.

John found a wrought-iron table at the back of

the café. It was tiny and seemed more suited to a streetside coffee shop, but it was the only table available. Charlotte slid into one chair while John disappeared to place their order.

John glanced her way as he waited in line. He gave her a little nod. What that meant, she couldn't say, but it unleashed a flurry of goosebumps down her back. She smiled in return, then dove for her water glass to relieve her parched throat. Why was she so nervous about this lunch? She'd completed dozens of assignments as a traveling doctor. Meeting new people, fitting in—it was all old news to her. So this edgy feeling she had around John made no sense.

It was also annoying, because she had some ideas for helping Angel get her testing done faster. She needed to stay focused if she was going to get past John's territorial tendencies, not stutter her way through her speech because of nerves.

Reflexively she groped through her handbag until her fingers found her lipstick and compact. She flipped it open to check her appearance and was just about to freshen her lipstick when she paused.

What are you doing, Char?

Her gaze shifted from the mirror to John, who had made it to the order counter and was oblivious to her gaze. He was a solidly built man, that was for sure, with a cool, streetwise vibe that the teens gravitated to. The woman taking his order was giving him lots of big smiles while twirling a strand of her hair. Even at this distance, it was obvious she was flirting.

Charlotte could see the appeal. John was a strong, attractive man, with a no-nonsense attitude that could make a girl feel a bit invincible by his side.

Her gaze shifted back to her mirror. Was that what she was doing too? Flirting a little with her attractive, vigilant colleague?

She paused to consider that scenario, then felt a rush of heat as she realized it was true. She snapped her compact shut. No need to give anyone the wrong idea—including herself. She had one simple rule when it came to romance on the road, designed to keep her career intact and her reputation stellar. *No. Dating. Coworkers.* As a traveling doctor, she needed excellent recommendations to secure her next assignment. She couldn't afford loose ends, bad breakups, or misunderstandings in her line of work.

So John could keep that stacked body of his on his side of the clinic—because romance was not in the cards.

Nor was it the point of this lunch!

She shook her head in frustration.

Focus, Charlotte.

She closed her eyes and mentally reviewed the lines she had practiced all week.

John, I know I'm only here for a few months. So, I hope you won't think I'm speaking out of turn when I say that I don't think we can just wait for Angel to be ready to trust us before we refer her for testing. There must be some other way to get her EKG done...something we can work out with the hospital. I don't know exactly how yet, but I'm just not willing to take no for an answer...

"Take no for an answer to what?"

John was back, holding two chilled fruit sodas in one hand and a basket of just-fried tortilla chips in the other. His bulky frame was less intimidating, now that it was paired with his relaxed, friendly smile.

Her flood of goosebumps returned, making her wonder if it really was nerves that made her body react this way.

Embarrassed, she grabbed a chip, eager for an excuse not to talk. "Mmm..." she said, waving her chip like an idiot. "Delicious!"

She moved over as far as she could to make room for him to settle into his chair, but his knee jammed hard against hers anyway. He muttered an apology as he moved left while she went right, both doing their best to navigate their postage stamp of a table. Despite their amateur gymnastics, she could still feel the heat of his leg next to hers, his jeans tickling her ankle. That set off another hot explosion of nervous energy that she couldn't seem to tame.

John used the heel of his hand to twist the metal caps from their glass bottles, then handed one to her. The strawberry-lime fizziness was a sweet, cool contrast to the salty chips. John took a deep draw from his soda, then set the bottle down to study her. She felt like a spotlight had suddenly been aimed her way, making her wish she had freshened up that lipstick after all.

"John…" she began—because that was the way she'd practiced it in front of her bathroom mirror that morning.

"I suppose I owe you an apology," he said, at the exact same moment.

"I know I'm only going to be at The Sunshine Clinic for a few… Wait…what?" she stuttered, flabbergasted that the prickly pediatrician she'd met a week ago was even capable of an apology.

He leaned in close enough to stir the hair at her temple when he spoke, launching her heart into a swift staccato.

"Listen, I probably shouldn't tell you this." He looked over both shoulders as if checking for eavesdroppers. "But The Sunshine Clinic…"

"Yes?"

"We're not really a medical clinic."

"What are you talking about?" Hints of sandalwood and orange spice from his aftershave were confusing her even more than this strange conversation.

"Remember those makeover shows? Where the show's producers took average people and gave them glamorous makeovers?"

She couldn't imagine where this was going. But it was interesting, so she grabbed another chip and waited.

"We're doing a show like that at the clinic. Hidden cameras and all that. But we're targeting medical professionals. It's called *Medical Makeovers 911* and you were our very first wardrobe intervention!" He leaned back in his chair, leaving a cool rush of air in his wake. "What did you think?"

His demeanor was typical Dr. J—calm, cool, unflappable. But there was an unmistakable glint of mischief in his gaze and she rather liked it.

She tapped her chin with one manicured fingernail, thinking fast on her feet. "Tackling the profession's lab coat problem? I see…"

"Exactly. They're so predictable."

She tilted her head, taking in this new, unexpected side of her colleague. So Dr. John Bennett had a sense of humor. Who would have guessed? Not her. But now she wanted to keep the game going, so she could tease out the smile making the corners of his mouth dance. "So donated cargo pants and faded tee shirts are…what? Med Chic?"

His eyes widened with delight at having a sparring partner. "Maybe Retro Rounding?"

"On-Call Casual? But wait…" She indicated his dark jeans and leather jacket with a wave of her hand. "What do you call this?"

"This?" He opened his jacket to check himself out. "I call this Hip-Hop Doc." Then he looked down at his red tee shirt, featuring a garish cartoon picture of a burrito. "With a side of kitsch."

She shook her head in mock disapproval. "Looks more like Grunge G.P. to me. With a side of goofy."

And then he laughed—a wondrous, husky sound that made Charlotte feel like she had won a fabulous prize. He tapped his bottle against hers.

"Touché. Sorry for the corny attempt at humor. Just my way of trying to make up for your first day getting off to such a rotten start. That was entirely my fault."

For the first time since she'd started working at the clinic, the pins-and-needles anxiety that she felt in John's presence faded. The whole world felt new and shiny, like Seattle's streets after a spring rainstorm. But dangerous too. Because it would be harder to stick to her No Dating Co-workers rule if her colleague was as charming as he was handsome.

She took a quick sip of her soda, hoping her attraction didn't show. "Well, it did seem like you were having a bad day."

John tilted his head with a soft half-smile.

"You were talking to someone when I came in," she clarified. "It didn't sound like it was going well."

He was thoughtful for a moment. "Oh, right! That was the principal at Piper's school." He dragged a hand down his face. "That kid's gonna be the death of me."

"I saw her picture on your desk. She doesn't look that scary."

"No?" He chuckled. "Try this on for size." He ticked a list off on his fingers. "Three schools and four nannies in seven months."

Charlotte finished her soda and set it aside. "She works fast. I'll give you that."

John's expression grew serious. "It's not her fault. My brother got himself into some trouble last year. He's been sentenced to five years in prison on drug charges. Because of that, my eleven-year-old niece must live with her bachelor uncle on his tiny sailboat."

Bachelor uncle.

So, he was single. Interesting...

Not interesting! Irrelevant!

"She doesn't even have a room to call her own. I've listed the boat for sale, and I have been looking for a new place. Something cozy, not too far from the clinic, with a little backyard where we can grow a few vegetables. Maybe even get a pet, like she's been begging for. But between my clinic hours and taking care of Piper, there hasn't been much time for house-shopping."

"So, that's why I'm here?" Charlotte deduced.

"That is indeed why you're here. Though I'm not used to sharing my turf with other doctors." He gave her a wry smile. "As you may have noticed."

"Yes, I may have noticed that," Charlotte agreed solemnly.

He tilted his soda bottle her way. "Enough about me. Just who exactly are you?"

"In case you've forgotten, I'm Dr. Charlotte Owens…"

He waved her off. "Not the boring stuff. I want to hear the good stuff. Like why a doctor who graduated top of her class has a resume full of locum assignments. And how you wound up in my little clinic, with nothing but an old wood door for your desk and a surly doctor in your face?"

She chuckled, enjoying their new camaraderie. "The old wood door is growing on me."

And maybe the surly doc was too.

She gave a casual shrug before delivering the canned description of her nomadic life that she had perfected over the years. "It's a great way to see the world…" *pause for a moment…* "without paying for an expensive hotel room!"

Perfect. Now laugh and toss your hair over your shoulder, just like the carefree girl you are.

John nodded but his gaze was serious, not quite joining in the fun. "So, you're a destination doc, then? I've read about that—doctors who use locum tenens assignments to see the world, complete with travel stipends and per diems for meals."

She shrugged. "It keeps the bills paid, right?" Charlotte reached for her soda again, but it was empty, which gave her hands nothing to do. "Just trying to keep life casual and fun, you know? No worries about hospital politics or micromanaging supervisors. I help where I'm needed, then spend my free time on the slopes or in the surf. The whole work-hard-play-hard thing, right?"

It was enough to leave it at that. He didn't need to know the truth. That she couldn't settle down in one place for long before she got an itchy sensation at the nape of her neck. Like a warning that something dangerous was headed her way. He didn't need to know why she couldn't have a favorite pie café, or a puppy, or spend the weekend painting her living room.

Because once upon a time, she'd had all those things, only to have them snatched away in the middle of the night by a police officer with a kind face who'd knocked on the door, then shattered her world.

She'd survived that once and learned how to live a life that couldn't be taken away.

Because she always left first.

By now people had usually asked all sorts of questions about her travels. Then told her how they wished they could go back in time, be a little more adventurous before the pressures of work and family settled them into rigid routines. That had inspired her to launch her travel blog, where she posted the pictures and stories of her travels around the world.

"I'm surprised you landed in Seattle," John said, his gaze intense and watchful. "Not exactly an international destination, is it? Unless you're an avid skier or snowboarder?"

Under different circumstances, Charlotte would have loved to take her snowboard out to one of Seattle's many ski runs. But that was not what this trip was about. "Seattle's my hometown, actually. I just came back because my father left me his house."

"I'm so sorry. I didn't realize you'd lost your father."

"Thanks, but I didn't really know him. He and my mom broke up before I was born."

John's brows narrowed. "Yet he left you his house? Why?"

It was a great question, but she had no idea why he'd left her his house. The letter the attorney had given her, with its promise of explanation, was still sitting in her kitchen, on top of the toaster oven where she had warmed her English muffin that morning.

"He never married or had more kids, so maybe I was his only choice."

That was just about all the personal chit-chat she cared to share. It was time to get back to the reason for this lunch—Angel's need for an EKG.

She took a deep breath. "John, I know I'm only here—"

"So it's just you and your mom, then? Or do you have siblings?"

The question stumped her for a minute. She couldn't understand why he was so interested in her family. "It was just me and my mom. But she died when I was thirteen, and I didn't have other family so I grew up in foster care."

Time to lead him back to safe territory. Where was their lunch, anyway?

"So, I've been thinking about Angel and—"

"What was she like? Your mom?"

Goodness, were they still talking about her? She'd much rather show him her latest social media posts, pictures of a mountain resort ski clinic in Colorado where she'd spent a month working. But something about his intense gaze made her doubt she could distract him so easily.

"She was...you know...nice. Like most moms are, I guess. Anyway, we don't have much time before we have to get back to the clinic, John, and I really think we should discuss—"

John leaned back in his chair and folded his arms in a relaxed, easygoing pose. "We've got plenty of time, Charlotte. All the time in the world, if we need it."

Charlotte bit her lip, out of ideas for how to get John to focus on anything but her. It was unnerving being the center of his attention. The way he was looking at her. Something about his gaze made the world feel like it had narrowed to just the two of them.

"Well, she was a single mom, you know. Things weren't easy for her...raising me on my own."

She waited for some kind of response, but he was placid, waiting for her to continue. She huffed an impatient sigh.

"We didn't have a lot of money, but I remember these silly little traditions she created for me. Like my birthday. Every year, on the night before my birthday, she'd let me stay up until midnight. We'd go to the local diner and have a midnight milkshake party so we could celebrate the exact moment I turned one year older."

These were memories she hadn't thought about for a long time. She smiled reflexively, remembering her mother's irrational excitement at sharing a simple milkshake with her.

John smiled in response, revealing a pretty irresistible dimple. "She sounds lovely, Charlotte."

Charlotte spun her empty soda bottle between her palms. "She was."

And I miss her a lot.

But she didn't want to dwell on that. Her life worked best when she stayed focused on the future, filling it with the destinations and assignments that kept her mind busy and her heart full.

She took a sip of water to regain her equilibrium. How did he do that? Somehow, in the space of five minutes, she had told John more about herself than she'd told anyone else. Unnerving, for sure.

It was high time to get back to the matter at hand. She cleared her throat and tried again. "John, I know I'm only here at The Sunshine Clinic for a few months—"

But then she felt a strange buzzing sensation under her hands, which she had splayed across the table.

"Sorry," John muttered, reaching for his cell phone. "Dr. Bennett speaking."

Maybe she should just send him an email. She was giving up hope that she and John were ever going to talk about Angel and how to pay for her EKG.

"Mm-hmm… Just a few hours, then?" John frowned and ran a hand through his hair. "Well, that's better than nothing, Cassie. And good luck with your exams!"

When he hung up, his relaxed vibe disappeared. He rubbed his forehead as if he had a headache. When he finally looked up, his face was tense in a way that was very un-Dr. J.

"That was my sitter," he explained. "I have been thinking about Angel's EKG. I want to be ready when she comes back to the clinic so we can get that test done quickly. We have a charity fund at the hospital that might cover Angel's testing. But the application is long, and I can't access her file away from the office, so I need to stay late to get it done. I was hoping my sitter would do a few nights this week, but she's studying for college entrance exams and can only give me one evening."

Just then, the server who'd taken John's order appeared with two red baskets. She was young and prettyand seemed to dawdle at their table just a bit too long, paying far more attention to John than was strictly necessary.

Charlotte could hardly blame the girl for flirting. John was a sexy catch and now, after chatting, she knew he had a heart of gold too. What girl wouldn't want to make a guy like John hers?

But that didn't justify the flare of jealousy that knotted her stomach. John was her colleague—and a temporary one at that. She shifted in her chair, trying to get comfortable, and that sent her knee crashing into John's again.

She should pull back into her tiny sliver of space.

But she didn't want to.

His leg was solid and warm. In some small way, her knee against his felt like she was laying claim to him. Even if it was just the claim of having a private lunch date.

"Nice to meet you," the server said, letting her hand trail against John's shoulder as she left.

Charlotte reached for another chip, desperate to burn off some angsty energy. But the basket was empty. John was watching her now, his expression both curious and challenging. But he didn't move away. If anything, his knee seemed to be returning the pressure.

What on earth was she doing? This was a working lunch—nothing more! Why on earth was she flirting with him?

She shifted her attention to her burrito, hiding any expression that would reveal the riot of emotions doing battle in her body. She tried to saw into her burrito with her plastic fork and knife, but the thick tortilla shell made a mockery of her efforts.

"That won't work. You gotta just go for it. Like this."

John demonstrated the technique by taking a huge bite of his burrito, making Charlotte regret her order. It was always awkward, eating in front of coworkers, but even more so when the stoic coworker in question had a smoldering sex appeal and was leaning his knee against hers.

She didn't want to think about that for too long, so she mimicked John's burrito technique, and the next thing she knew she had unleashed a hot, delicious mess of charbroiled pork and spicy red sauce all over her fingers. Before she could blush again, John laughed with abandon, making everything—the stress of her new job, the messy burrito, her unexpected jealousy—seem miraculous and wonderful.

She couldn't help but join in. Maybe everything was going to be okay. Surely these strange reactions to John would quiet down soon, and they would settle into a sensible friendship.

But then John passed her a stack of napkins, and his fingers grazed hers. That was when she knew she was wrong. Terribly, horribly wrong. Because that barely noticeable touch sent a hot charge of electricity racing from her fingertips to some place deep in her core. The sensation was not friendly. It was hot and demanding...impossible to ignore.

She couldn't downplay her body's reactions to John anymore. There was something about him that sent her body into a mutinous riot every time he was near.

Charlotte had a sudden unbidden image of John working alone after hours in the dark clinic, with nothing but empty takeout containers to keep him company. The urge to offer her help was so powerful she had to bite her lip to keep herself in check. Staying after-hours at the clinic with a colleague she found insanely attractive was a terrible idea. Quite possibly the worst idea of her life. If she wanted to get back some semblance of self-control, she needed to keep her distance and stick strictly to business. No more lunches alone, no more talk of anything other than clinic business, and certainly no being alone with John after hours.

No. Dating. Colleagues. Remember that simple but oh-so-effective rule, Charlotte?

John wadded up his napkin and placed it in the now-empty basket. "Well, it was just an idea. We'll just have to hope that Angel finds her way back to the clinic soon and is ready to give us her real name."

That was a long shot and they both knew it. But obviously John was concerned for Angel too and had found a way to get her EKG covered. Without charity funding, there was little they could do for Angel unless she literally collapsed on the street and needed emergency care.

So, while keeping her distance might keep Charlotte's heart safe, it would do nothing for Angel, who was at a great deal more risk.

"I could help," Charlotte blurted, and then squeezed her eyes shut, wondering if John would be shocked at her boldness.

But John didn't look shocked. If anything, he seemed pleased. "Are you sure?"

Invisible hands pushed her from behind.

Go for it! some long-dormant voice screamed in her head. *You know you like him. Maybe something good will happen.*

Or maybe things would end badly and she would ruin her professional reputation.

But her next assignment was already set, and the tiny dimples that shadowed his smile were making all her reasons pop like bubbles in the sun.

"Yeah, I'm sure," she said quickly, before she could change her mind.

CHAPTER FOUR

JOHN SURVEYED THE preparations for his after-hours meeting with Charlotte. For the millionth time, he wished for a proper conference room, or even just an office.

Rome wasn't built in a day.

For Pete's sake, Rome wasn't his problem right now. What *was* his problem were these jittery, restless feelings that were driving him mad as his workday ended. He was spending entirely too much time double-checking that he had every form and supply they could possibly need. Not to mention stressing about whether he should order dinner in, or if that would look too much like a date.

Because this wasn't a date. This was strictly two professionals collaborating on a difficult case.

Oh, what a load of bunk. He spent entirely too much time thinking about Charlotte to believe that he wasn't interested. Of course he was interested—what man in his right mind wouldn't be interested in Charlotte? She was beautiful and smart, naturally warm, and adventurous. With little hints of vulnerability that she thought she kept hidden. So endearing.

Before John could stress on any more details, Charlotte showed up.

"Very efficient," she said, nodding to the supplies he had organized with military precision.

She brushed his shoulder as she passed, and the faint hint of her touch, plus her unique jasmine-infused scent, did nothing to quiet his nerves. If anything, her proximity set off an increasingly familiar war between his heart and his head, with his heart taking a strong lead today.

Sarah appeared in the doorway. "Do you two need anything before I go?"

It was kind of her to offer. But, as much as John appreciated Sarah's help, he also craved time alone with Charlotte, without the constant interruption of phone calls and texts and questions and emergencies. Even their lunch date had been a noisy, cramped affair, but it had also been intriguing. He couldn't stop thinking about the press of her knee against his. Had that been intentional? Maybe not. That table had been tiny—it was probably just logistics.

But he didn't think so. There had been something challenging and exciting in her eyes when their knees touched, and he strongly suspected she had been flirting.

That possibility had haunted his thoughts ever since the lunch and he was beyond annoyed with himself. He needed to focus on Angel's funding, not wonder if Charlotte had the hots for him. In another time and space, yes—he would pursue Charlotte with all he had. But that time and head-space belonged to Piper now, and it wasn't fair to start something with Charlotte that was destined to end badly.

The lunch date had been good. They had broken the ice and were on a friendlier footing now. No need to hope for anything more than that.

John separated the application form and handed her half. "We don't have much time, so I thought we could each take half and help each other as needed. I've got to warn you, though—this could take some time."

As John handed her a pen, a terrible thought occurred to him. Seattle was Charlotte's hometown, surely full of friends, classmates, and maybe a former lover or two?

The sudden hot rush of raw jealousy that roiled in his gut was ridiculous, but he had to ask anyway. "Unless you need to leave soon because someone is waiting?"

Charlotte's pen stilled, but she didn't look up.

"Nope," she said, and it seemed a bit too cheerful in John's opinion. "No one is waiting for me."

Good grief, what was wrong with him? The rush of relief he felt was just wrong. Someone like Charlotte should not go home to an empty house. She was beautiful, and smart, with a huge, warm heart for teens like Angel. But he couldn't deny that it pleased him to know that she was free. John had his faults, but dishonesty wasn't one of them.

Charlotte and her pen got back to work. He should do the same. But his mind was in a state of mutiny and his gaze lingered on her profile. He felt an invisible current buzzing between them that made him hyper aware of everything about her. The heat of her body, the rise and fall of her chest, the way she pursed her lips just so when she worked… His gaze lingered just a breath too long and she looked up to catch him staring.

Time froze for a moment, maybe two, before she gifted him a sweet, spontaneous smile. Then she shook her head in a scolding fashion and glanced him with her elbow.

"Come on, lazy bones. Get back to work."

A very sensible idea. He should totally do that. But the black squiggly marks on the pages before him could not compete with Charlotte for his attention. He shook his head to clear the fog.

"So, how did you end up living on a sailboat?" she asked. "It sounds quite romantic."

He laughed, thinking of his tiny living space, anchored just feet from his neighbors, with the constant briny scent of old boats and sea water.

"It started as a way to save money on rent while I was in med school. And I don't know about romantic… Last week I had the scare of my life. I woke up in the wee hours of the morning to a terrible commotion on the deck. I thought someone was trying to break in! Piper hid in the bathroom while I went to check it out, baseball bat in hand."

Charlotte waited, her eyes wide. "What happened?"

He laughed. "It was just a sea lion, looking for shelter from predators. Or a free meal."

"A case of barking and entering, then?"

"You could say that." He chuckled.

She shook her head as she refocused on the paperwork before her. "You know, in all the travel adventures and mishaps I've written about on my blog, I don't believe I have a sailing story. Maybe I could interview you sometime? Get a few pictures and put it on my blog?"

Before John could think it through, he blurted, "Better than that—I'll take you sailing!"

Her laugh was spontaneous and relaxed. "That would be great."

John was sorely tempted to bang his head against the table a few times. Maybe that was what it would take to knock some sense into him.

He quickly changed the conversation to keep himself out of trouble.

"But, as much as I love sailing, *The House Call* is no place for a tween girl to grow up. She needs privacy and space…a backyard. Even that pet she's been begging for."

And as much as he hated the idea of being anchored to a mortgage and property taxes, Piper's need for stability was more important than his whimsical dreams of adventure.

He hated it, but a familiar pang of nostalgia roiled in his gut. Nostalgia for his life before Piper, when he had been free to live as he pleased. With his mother gone and his brother grown, it had felt like the past was finally behind him. Finally, it was time for him to pursue his own dreams, with no fear of hurting or disappointing anyone.

But, like the Greek god Icarus, his dreams had taken him too close to the sun, searing his wings until they could hold him no more. It was his brother, though, not him, who'd crashed to the earth, no longer buoyed up by John's promise to be his keeper.

What a terrible thing it was…watching others pay for his mistakes.

Charlotte laid her pen down and tilted her head. "So, do I have this right? You started to take care of your brother when you were probably still wearing action hero pajamas. Then you started a clinic to make sure Seattle's homeless teens received good medical care. And now you're raising your niece."

He felt hypnotized by those indigo-blue eyes. Utterly incapable of looking away.

"I have to ask…" She leaned forward, and the slight movement was enough to stir the air between them, filling the space with her intriguing jasmine scent. "Just who takes care of Dr. J?"

Long-buried emotions rumbled deep in his gut. Her question touched a soft, raw place in his heart that was best left alone. In all the years he had tried to fill his father's shoes no one had ever asked about him, or the sacrifices he'd had to make. When kids his age had been buzzing about baseball tryouts or running off to spend a hot summer day at the nearby creek, he'd had to focus on his little family, making sure Michael was safe so his mother could work hard… so hard…making sure they had a roof over their head and some food in the refrigerator. It had never occurred to him to want more. Or maybe it had and he'd just learned to be numb long ago. Because there hadn't ever been any "more" to be had.

Charlotte was waiting patiently for answers he didn't have. Everything about her felt receptive and warm. She wanted to know him—and, as much of a revelation as that was, it was even more of one to realize he wanted to be known by her.

He coughed and shifted in his chair. "No one, I guess. It's just me and Piper."

"And before that just you and your brother?"

He nodded. It was just the three of them when his dad had skipped out, leaving his mom three months behind on rent and a boatload of bills. But he didn't want to dive into all that. It was getting late, and he wanted to focus on Angel's application—not the mess of responsibilities that his father had left on his young shoulders.

When they'd finished the application John walked Charlotte to her car, grateful for her help but still haunted by her question.

"Just who takes care of Dr. J?"

All his life he'd done his best to fill the void his father's absence had left behind. It was second nature for him to take care of Michael, the teens, and now Piper…to make sure she didn't fall into the same abyss as her father.

He had no regrets for his decisions so far, but was this his destiny? It often seemed that way. He was Piper's guardian for the next few years. Then Michael would return and need help getting his life back on track. The clinic would always need him to fight for money and resources. And someday Sarah would retire, leaving him without a trusted partner to figure this out.

Charlotte glanced up at him as they walked. She was wearing a wool pea coat, dark leggings, and black boots. Her hair was pulled up in her trademark messy bun that left tendrils of loose curls framing her face. Beneath the weak lighting of the parking lot's lamps, her blue eyes were as dark and stormy as the sea he loved. She gave him a little smile and then he knew. He wasn't imagining things, and her knee against his had not been an accident. That electric buzz he felt when she was near…? She felt it too. He was sure of it.

Her car chirped twice as she unlocked it with her remote and the interior lights came on. She arranged her things in the passenger seat, then met him at the driver's side. She reached for the door handle, then paused and turned back, her eyes wide with questions. She seemed less confident out here in the dark, just the two of them alone, the moment full of possibility.

Her question still lingered in his heart. What about him? When *would* it be his turn to find happiness?

He stepped forward, drawn to her warmth, wanting to touch her, hold her. Maybe now was his time. Right now…with her.

His cell phone beeped twice—the distinctive tone that signaled a text from his sitter. A sign that he was lingering too long in this quiet space with Charlotte. And a reminder of what was at stake. He was Piper's guardian because of the mistakes he had made with her father. He had to do better by Piper. He just had to.

Maybe later would be his time. When Michael came home. Or when Piper was older.

His jaw clenched with frustration. Yes, that was what he had. A whole basket of *maybes* to keep him warm at night.

Charlotte was practically in his arms, her gaze raking his face, trying to make sense of the emotions he couldn't hide. But as much as he wanted to feel her warm body against his, he needed to do the right thing—because following his desires would only hurt her in the end. After years of practice, he thought he'd become numb to the resentment of turning his back on what he wanted. But the effort of leaving Charlotte had his fingers curling into tight, hard fists.

Deep breath. Count to three. Then open the car door and send her off with a brisk goodnight.

Quick and painless. Like ripping off a Band-Aid.

But in the end his body betrayed him. He found himself bending to graze her lips with a featherlight kiss, stealing something small and warm for himself. Her lips were soft and receptive, a safe harbor on this bitterly cold night. His hand wandered of its own accord, finding her hair, then her neck, trailing over it with his fingers, setting loose a flurry of goosebumps in his wake. Her gloved hand found and grasped his, as if steadying herself. How his body raged for more—a deeper kiss, a longer night…

But he had to put a stop to this. He'd already gone too far.

"I'm sorry," he whispered, though he lacked the strength to explain why.

Before his heart could make more trouble, he turned on his heel and strode back to the clinic. An icy wind kicked up, slicing through his thin tee shirt and raking his face with its cruel, cold claws.

Her car door slammed, making him pause at the clinic's entrance. When her engine revved, he fought off the urge to call her back. Instead, he channeled his frustration into a ferocious pull on the clinic door that made it bang against the cement support post with a satisfying crack.

Then he ducked back into the clinic.

Back where he belonged.

Charlotte stopped by the coffee station before her last appointment of the day. It had been a long, grueling day, thanks to an influenza outbreak.

But Sarah had made things a little better by leaving a basket of home-baked treats near the coffee pot.

Charlotte was unwrapping an enticing blueberry muffin when she heard John approach. Her spine spontaneously stiffened at the sound of his footsteps.

All weekend she had been unable to escape her thoughts of John and that phantom kiss. She could still feel how his lips had brushed hers, so light she'd wondered if it was a dream.

It made her feel foolish to be thinking this way, unable to shake thoughts of him no matter what she tried. Her weekend had been a frenzy of cleaning and organizing, followed by long runs through the upscale neighborhood of her father's home. All so she could escape the awful yearning that his teasing kiss had left behind.

But even when she had worn herself out she'd still been able to remember the way she'd felt, pressed to John's chest. Like he was a mighty fortress, sheltering her from harm.

This must stop.

That was what she had vowed that morning on her way to work. She needed to come to her senses and put a stop to whatever this was between them. Infatuation? A crush? Whatever. They were both adults with sexual needs. Obviously they had developed some harmless attraction. So what? Attractions weren't destiny. They could be fun, or they could be annoying, but they were always meaningless so long as you didn't act on them.

From now on she would stick to her side of the clinic. No more lunches with John. No more after-hours work sessions. She would just focus on her patients and confer with John only when absolutely necessary.

And now here he was, standing behind her, his breath stirring her hair. Ready or not, it was time to put her new resolve to the test.

"Afternoon," John said. "How was your weekend?"

He reached across her for the cream and sugar packets, sending notes of sandalwood and citrus into her space. Her traitorous body went on full alert, forcing her to close her eyes against the rush of desire.

Sticking to her side of the clinic was going to be a challenge.

"Very busy," she croaked.

Her hamstrings still ached from the long miles she had logged, trying to outrun her thoughts of him.

For a long minute John doctored his coffee with two creams and one sugar, as was his habit. Charlotte willed herself back to her office, where she'd be safely sheltered from his tempting masculine aura. But her body seemed frozen in place, forcing her into an inner battle of self-control.

Just when she'd mustered enough willpower to grab her coffee cup and leave, he stopped her with a question.

"Do you have a moment? There's something I'd like to discuss."

Alone? In your office?

Her resolve was too new and shiny for this level of challenge!

"Of course," she whispered.

She followed him on autopilot, trying to ignore how the soft, well-washed denim of his jeans hugged every masculine curve of his backside.

He closed the door behind her. For one wild moment she thought he might push her up against the wall, crush her mouth with his, and finish what he'd started in the parking lot last week.

And if he did? Would she politely demur and explain her new sensible plan for self-preservation?

No, she would not do that. She would lose her ever-loving mind—that she was sure of. And then she would need a new plan.

What on earth was wrong with her? Vowing to retreat one minute…willing to toss the rules out the window the next.

Casual and fun!

That was her motto when it came to romance.

Easy-breezy, no promises, no demands.

But when it came to John, what she felt was anything but casual or fun. It was intense and greedy...like a wild animal she couldn't control.

John leaned against his exam table. She stood near the door and felt a brief impulse to bolt before things got any more complicated.

She took a deep breath to steady herself.

It was just a silly little kiss, she chided herself. *He probably doesn't even remember it.*

"Thanks for your time," John said. He crossed his arms over his chest, making his leather jacket strain against his bulky arms. "We should talk about what happened last week. After we finished Angel's application."

Crap. He wanted to talk about the kiss.

"Okay," she whispered.

"I was out of line, kissing you like that. I apologize for being inappropriate, and I genuinely hope I didn't make you uncomfortable."

Uncomfortable? No, sir.

There were a lot of things that kiss had made her feel, but uncomfortable was not one of them.

"Listen, Charlotte... I hope I'm not out of line to say this. You're a beautiful woman, and I'm very attracted to you."

She bit her lip, unsure how to respond. Of course, she knew he felt something for her—that was obvious from the kiss. But hearing him say it out loud…even the way her name rolled off his lips…she felt a strong desire to throw the rules out the window and just let her body take the lead.

The only thing that stopped her was his expression. He didn't look like a hopeful lover confessing his feelings. More like a fugitive confessing his crimes.

"But I have Piper in my life now. She's still adjusting to the trauma of what happened with her father. It's just a terrible time for me to be…"

Charlotte felt her heart sink. Which made no sense since she had come to work determined to keep her distance from John.

But there was a tiny piece of her heart that had spent the weekend wondering if John had thought of her half as much as she had obsessed over him.

And now she knew. He *had* been thinking about her. A lot.

About what a mistake it had been to kiss her.

He didn't want her in his bed, or maybe even in his life.

She could practically feel her heart latching every window and bolting every door. Every beat screamed *Mayday! Mayday! Mayday!* as her body stiffened for battle.

She jutted out her chin and sharpened her

sword. "It's fine," she said coolly. "I didn't think it meant anything. In fact, I hardly remember it."

John stuffed his hands in his pockets and looked down at his shoes. "Right… I'm glad you understand."

Charlotte fought off the urge to snort. She understood just fine.

Inconvenient. Unwanted. Go away.

Sarah knocked and poked her head around the door. "Sorry to interrupt. Dr. Owens, your patient is ready." Then her gaze ping-ponged between them. "Unless you want me to reschedule?"

Charlotte pushed herself off the wall. "No need, Sarah. I think we're done here."

So done.

But she couldn't help but steal a glance at John. He had his back to her, hands still stuffed deep in his leather jacket as he looked out the window. She heard his long, audible sigh just before she left.

He was probably relieved that it was over.

Well, she was too. This was what she got for even *thinking* about breaking the rule that had kept her heart safe all these years.

Lesson learned—thankfully before any real damage had been done. She should be dancing a jig down the hall. *GypsyMD* was a free-spirited gal. No strings holding her down, thank you very much.

But instead of relief or joy she was left with a bitter taste in her mouth and one burning question.

Why did getting what she wanted feel so bad?

CHAPTER FIVE

CHARLOTTE STOPPED BY the coffee station for the cup of coffee she hadn't got. Drat, the pot was empty. She didn't have time to make another, so she headed to her exam room where Sam, a fifteen-year-old boy complaining of headaches, was waiting.

Sarah had put an asterisk next to the symptoms, which was her way of signaling that the teen was making a complaint about one thing but probably needed to be seen for something else. This sometimes happened when a patient had a private concern or didn't know exactly what they needed.

Sam was seated on the exam table facing the door when Charlotte entered. He wore combat boots and camouflage pants—the sort of things he could find at a military surplus store. His sweatshirt was zipped up, the hood pulled far over his head. It looked like he had created a safe cocoon for himself.

"Hey, Sam."

She was about to ask about his headaches when she noticed a strong odor in the room. Infection? Poor hygiene? No, more like decay. And the closer she got to the thin boy with the big brown eyes, the stronger the scent was.

"So, Sarah tells me you're not feeling well."

Over the past few weeks Charlotte had learned to keep her questions open-ended, even if her patient had written something specific on their intake form. It allowed the teen more space to share what was wrong, and often one symptom was really three or four.

The boy bit his lip and looked away. "My feet hurt."

"Okay. Let's get those boots off so I can take a look."

Charlotte kept her voice as light and casual as she could, trying to distract herself from the overpowering odor. Her brain was already reviewing the possibilities. He could have an out-of-control fungal infection. Or boots that needed to be replaced. Maybe a bacterial infection that had gotten out of hand.

The boy just sat there, looking straight down at the floor, not moving. His hood was draped over his face now, hiding him from the world and from her.

She washed her hands slowly, planning how to proceed. Charlotte was accustomed to having parents in the room with her patients, who could provide a full medical history and ensure compliance. But here it was just her and Sam.

Her first instinct was to lecture him about all the bad things that might happen if she didn't treat whatever problem he had. But nothing about his body language or demeanor said that he was resistant or rebellious.

Instead, he looked ashamed—which broke her heart. Why should he feel one second of shame for something that wasn't his fault?

What would John do?

She was surprised when that thought jumped into her head, considering how infuriated she'd been with him just a few minutes ago. But whatever her personal issues were with John, he was a hero to the teens who came to the clinic. They trusted him implicitly, and he'd earned that trust by being honest and reliable. If John were here, he wouldn't lecture Sam—that was for sure. He would slow things down…way down…so it seemed like he had all the time in the world to spend with the boy.

That was probably why he was always running late. But it was also why the teens trusted him so much.

Time to borrow a page from John's playbook.

"Sam, I'm going to take your boots off now, okay?"

Charlotte took one foot in her hands. Sam didn't resist or pull away, so she felt she was on the right track. The boot was old, and very worn, the sole pulling away from the upper. She untied the laces slowly. She would have liked to keep up a steady stream of mindless chit-chat to set his mind at ease.

So, how's school? What's your favorite subject? Do you have any pets?

But none of those questions felt right. She didn't know if Sam had a bed of his own, let alone pets or the ability to get to school every day.

As soon as she tried to remove his boot, she saw Sam's first problem. The boots were at least two sizes too small for him. As she tugged and pulled on the boot Sam winced in obvious pain.

"My goodness, Sam! How do you get these off every day?"

He shot her a deer-in-the-headlights look. That was when she realized he probably didn't take his boots off every day. Because it was too painful.

"I'm sorry…this might hurt a bit. You ready?"

He peered at her through long bangs, fear shadowing his eyes.

"I promise you'll feel better when this is done. Okay?"

He bit his lip, then looked away. He gave her a faint nod again.

She applied steady, even pressure as she pulled

and wiggled. Eventually the boot gave way—at the same time Sam cried out in pain. Any feeling of triumph that she might have felt at winning the boot war was instantly overshadowed by waves of the strong smell of infection. Charlotte forced herself not to react. Sam knew darn well the odor was coming from him. He didn't need her to remind him.

"Okay, Sam, one more time."

She repeated the process for his other boot, then began her assessment.

Sam's socks were in tatters, barely covering the sores that covered his feet. The sores had broken down the skin and were causing tissue loss, which was the source of the odor. She couldn't imagine how Sam managed to get around on feet that were in this condition.

Charlotte could feel Sam's eyes on her, fearing judgement or ridicule. This, she realized, was the moment when John had the most impact on the teens. When someone had revealed their greatest source of shame and pain, what did you say?

She slowly and gently released his feet, then looked up at him, feeling the weight of the world—Sam's world—on her shoulders. He just wanted to hear that everything would be okay. That was all any of the teens who came to the clinic wanted.

Charlotte shrugged and smiled. "I can fix this, Sam. No problem."

Sam bit his lip again, then nodded and visibly relaxed. Charlotte started by soaking his feet in an Epsom bath to help with the inflammation. He had a severe case of trench foot—a condition she'd honestly never expected to see outside of a medical textbook. But it made sense. Winter was Seattle's rainy season. And, while Charlotte loved to listen to the sounds of a rainstorm while she cooked dinner or read a book by the fire, days of rain were a nightmare for homeless teens. Their clothing, sleeping bags and footwear all got soaked. If they didn't have a safe, dry place to go, and extra pairs of dry socks and shoes, this was what happened.

She gently toweled his feet off, avoiding the blisters. "Does this hurt, Sam?"

He shook his head. "Not really. My feet used to hurt a lot, but then I decided to keep my boots on all the time. Pretty soon I stopped feeling anything at all."

That was not a good sign. Losing feeling meant his feet had been wet long enough to cause damage to his circulation and nerve function. As he healed, the feeling would return with a vengeance, which meant days of intense pain.

Charlotte sprayed his feet with antibiotic, then handed him a pair of new, clean socks. "I'm going to give you several pairs of dry socks, Sam, and we'll find some shoes that fit you from our donation box. You're going to need to keep your feet clean and dry, so they can heal. I'll make sure you get some antibiotic spray, too, and some pain relievers. I'd like to see you again next week, if that's all right?"

"Sure."

He slid off the table and gingerly landed on his feet. She handed him a pair of throwaway slippers to wear with his socks. Not a fashionable look, but that was probably all he could handle until his feet were in better shape.

"The best thing is to keep your feet clean, elevated, and exposed to the air for healing. Are you staying someplace where you can be warm and dry, Sam? In a shelter, maybe? Couch surfing with friends?"

His lips were a flat, tight line again as he shook his head.

"Let's go see Sarah, then. She has a way of finding shelter space when no one else can."

Sam's medical needs would help him get placed higher on the waiting lists too. With any luck he'd have a safe place to be while Social Services worked on finding a longer-term solution for him.

Charlotte left Sam with Sarah, after a hug and

a reminder to schedule his follow-up for the following week.

Sarah looked more frantic than usual. "Oh, honey, have you heard the news?"

"No?"

"It's Piper. She's had some kind of accident at school. John dashed off to meet the ambulance at the hospital. I'm afraid it's too late to have an on-call doctor fill in. Can you manage these last appointments on your own?"

There were two teens in the waiting area. One was stretched out on the vinyl chairs, grabbing a nap, while the other flipped through the pages of a magazine that was probably two years old.

"Of course—but what happened?"

"I don't know yet. John tore out of here twenty minutes ago." She waved her cell phone. "I'm going to wrap things up here, then head to the hospital. Want me to wait for you? Or will you meet us there?"

Charlotte froze with uncertainty. No matter how angry she had been at his apparent rejection of her as a romantic partner, she knew how much John loved his niece. Seeing her injured and in pain was probably killing him.

But that didn't mean he wanted her at the hospital. He'd made it clear that they were workmates, nothing more.

"I'm not sure yet," Charlotte said, still not able

to give a firm no. Because, as much as she wanted to push him away, she couldn't forget how he'd looked when he'd ended their kiss that night at the clinic. And that strange apology that didn't make sense… Was he really sorry he had kissed her? Or sorry that he had to stop?

She didn't have to decide right now. She could see these last two patients while Sarah went to John. Maybe Piper's accident wasn't that serious. Or maybe John would make his intentions known with a text or a phone call.

Sarah promised to let her know any news, then left for the hospital. Charlotte locked the front door behind her before returning to her exam room. She tried to focus on her last two patients, hoping that work would be her refuge from intrusive thoughts about John. Her heart might be closed off to any romantic entanglements with him, but that didn't mean she didn't care. He was a genuinely good man, who gave his best to everyone who counted on him. He deserved the support of friends at a time like this.

But did she belong at the hospital while he was facing a crisis? Well, the answer to that was probably no. He hadn't texted her since he'd left the clinic.

Besides, this was a family emergency—and she wasn't family. That was the price of being the Queen of Easy-Breezy. No messy commitments...no risk of loss. Just the way she liked it. But it also meant that no one ever thought to call on her for help, because she was always on her way somewhere else.

After she'd seen her patients, she locked up the clinic and headed to her car. It was strange, not seeing John's black SUV in its usual parking spot.

He's fine. You're fine. Everybody's fine. Just go home.

But it was impossible to imagine being back in her huge, empty house with a takeout order. Acting like it was just a normal night.

But that was what he wanted. For them to be just colleagues. That was what they both wanted.

You can't have your cake and eat it too, Owens.

A funny little phrase that meant she had to accept the limits of being colleagues. A sensible and wholly unsatisfying arrangement.

She made her way through the parking lot to the exit. Turned her left-hand signal on and waited for an opening in the traffic.

And then her phone chimed.

A text message. From John.

Hey.

That was all.

It was enough. She changed her turn signal from left to right and headed to the hospital.

* * *

Charlotte found John in the pediatric waiting room. Her heart gave an involuntary squeeze when she saw his bulky frame folded into a hard plastic chair. His eyes were closed, and he had his head resting on one hand, a day's worth of beard shadowing his jaw. All traces of the calm, cool and collected doctor she worked with every day were gone. He just looked weary and vulnerable.

She touched him lightly on the knee. "John?"

He woke up, dazed, looking at his surroundings in confusion.

Charlotte slid into the chair next to him. "What happened?"

John rubbed his eyes. "Bike accident at school. Piper was messing around, I guess, and went over the handlebars. Compound fracture of her fibula." He sighed and leaned back in his chair, the very image of weary exhaustion. "She'll need to stay a night or two for observation after her surgery, to make sure she doesn't have head trauma too. Then I can take her home."

Sarah appeared with a tray laden with mugs of coffee and half a Boston cream pie. Charotte had worked at the clinic long enough to know that in Sarah's worldview, there wasn't a problem in the world that couldn't be improved with hot coffee and a slice of pie.

"Home?" Sarah snorted. "To what? That sardine can you call home?"

"Yes, back to *The House Call*. Where else?" John clutched his coffee mug like it was a life preserver.

Sarah was having none of it. "That is a terrible place for Piper to recover. She has a broken leg, for Pete's sake! How is she going to get on and off the boat?"

"I'll help her."

Sarah rolled her eyes. "And what about bathing? She needs a bathtub where she can soak but keep her leg elevated and dry. And how comfortable is she going to be on a tiny little berth instead of a real, soft bed? What about the damp? And the mold?"

Sarah made good points. Charlotte had seen firsthand at the clinic how much longer it took their patients to recover from viruses and injuries because they didn't have the right environment to rest and recover.

Just then Charlotte looked up to find Sarah pinning her with a pointed stare. A *very* pointed stare.

"If only John had a friend with a spare bedroom or two. That sure would be helpful."

Charlotte felt her eyebrows dart upwards. Good grief, was Sarah suggesting that John and Piper stay with her?

No. That was crazy. Especially after they had just agreed to stay in their professional lanes. She and John barely knew each other. And Piper didn't know her at all. It would be strange, and awkward, and the complete opposite of keeping their distance as they had agreed.

It would also be helpful and kind and generous. All the things she had wanted this forced trip back to Seattle to be about.

Sarah was right. She had heard Charlotte complain enough about her father's home and its endless renovations. Every problem solved seemed to reveal two more. But renovations or not, the house was massive, with plenty of room for John and Piper. They could even have their own bathrooms, complete with luxurious marble baths and heated floor tiles.

She had no excuse not to offer the use of her home—except for her bruised ego and her desire to keep complications to a bare minimum.

She took a deep breath, then jumped in with both feet. "You could stay with me."

John looked up from his coffee, stunned and confused.

"My father's house—I mean, my house. It's huge and… Well, wait…"

She found her phone and navigated to the professional photos her real estate agent had sent a few days earlier in preparation for the house sale.

She flipped through the photos with John. "There's a bedroom off the kitchen that would be perfect for Piper, with its own bathroom. I could ask the work crew to add handrails to the bathtub if you want." She scrolled to the photos of the owner's suite. "And you could have this room…just down the hall from Piper."

"I don't know, Charlotte. This seems…"

"Weird?"

Because it was. It was extremely weird to invite a coworker of any kind, let alone one she had kissed and then agreed to avoid, to share her home for a few weeks.

He smiled. "Yes, but I was thinking more that it's an imposition."

"Not really. Honestly, the house is so huge I'll probably hardly know you're there."

Oh, so not true.

She would be acutely aware of his presence, but he didn't need to know that.

"I don't know… Maybe I could find a short-term rental for a month or two."

"Oh, John," Sarah huffed, crossing her arms across her chest. "You are not going to find a short-term two-bedroom rental on short notice. Stop being such a stubborn mule."

Emotions played out on John's face like a movie screen.

Stubborn, protective, uncertain, confused.

She knew what he was feeling because she felt it too. Inviting him to stay with her after they'd agreed to ignore their attraction felt like asking for trouble. But there were bigger issues at play than their feelings.

"Listen, John. This house I've inherited… Well, it's complicated. Let's just say that I've learned that my father chose his wealth over me when I was young. So I have resented the hell out of this house and all the suffering it represents for me and my mom."

She spontaneously grabbed his hand for emphasis, feeling strength in his broad palm and fingers.

"Using the house to help you and Piper would make me so happy. In some small way, it would make up for my father's selfishness, if that makes sense."

John's eyes were full of questions that she couldn't possibly answer right now.

He opened his mouth to protest, but then his shoulders slumped in resignation. "Maybe you're right. It would be good for Piper."

For the second time that day Charlotte got her way, yet she felt no sense of triumph. Already her emotions were a jumble of attraction and fear of getting hurt. Sure, they had agreed to keep things professional, but that was going to be a lot harder if John was showering and sleeping and living just down the hall from her.

A doctor in green scrubs approached. "Dr. Bennett?"

John jumped to his feet. "That's me."

"Piper's out of surgery. Everything went very well. Would you like to see her?"

"Yes, please!" He turned back to Charlotte. "One more thing… Thank you."

The next thing she knew he had drawn her to him, enfolding her in a warm hug that seemed to narrow the world down to just the two of them. She tried to return the hug like a friendly co-worker would, but when she felt the tension coiled in the muscles of his back her hands just itched to massage his worry away.

"For everything," he whispered against her ear.

Then he released her and followed the surgeon, leaving her to wonder what else he was grateful for.

CHAPTER SIX

How HAD HE made such a mess of things?

Charlotte's kitchen was in total chaos. John had used every surface to make the dough and homemade sauce for his infamous pizza recipe. The kitchen was warm and infused with the tantalizing aroma of cheese and pepperoni. The price of his efforts was flour spilled on the floor and tomato sauce splashed on the counter.

But that wasn't the mess he was worried about.

That particular complication was still at the clinic. He and Piper had moved into Charlotte's home during the day, while Charlotte was at work. Because he had taken family leave as soon as Piper was injured, he had not seen Charlotte since the night at the hospital when she'd invited him and Piper to stay with her while Piper recovered.

That must have been so uncomfortable for her. He knew Sarah had strongarmed her into the invitation. It was for Piper's sake that he'd agreed to stay, but he was still looking for a short-term rental. It was the right thing to do—especially since he had made such a huge deal about sticking to the boundaries of their working relationship.

What a hard conversation that had been. The last thing he'd wanted was for Charlotte to feel he was rejecting her—he wasn't! And he didn't want her to think he regretted that kiss. He just regretted the timing. Had they met last year— or a few years later, when Michael was reunited with his daughter—maybe a relationship would have worked out.

But Piper had to come first. She was just a kid, trying to make sense of a world that had turned upside down on her. If he hadn't gotten so caught up in his dream of starting The Sunshine Clinic maybe he would have seen the signs that his brother was in trouble. It was his fault that Piper had lost the dad she loved with all her heart, if only temporarily. He couldn't take the chance that surrendering to his chemistry with Charlotte might make him miss signs of trouble with Piper too.

But he could at least apologize for making such a mess of things with Charlotte. Hopefully his homemade pizza and a nice bottle of Chianti would smooth things over. Put them back on good footing as colleagues and hopefully even friends.

"More pizza?"

Piper didn't even look up. She was sitting on

one of the stools that flanked the kitchen bar. She had a laptop balanced on her lap and her leg, now wrapped in a new white cast, was propped on the chair next to her. Her fingers flew over her keyboard as she played some online game.

He sighed, missing the chatty girl he'd used to visit in California. There was little chance she'd want to watch a movie or play a board game with him tonight. Not with the fate of the universe playing out on her computer screen.

The oven alarm went off, signaling that the last pizza was done. This one was for Charlotte—his attempt to mimic the spinach and feta pizza she sometimes ordered for lunch at the clinic. Not quite as obvious as a big bouquet of flowers, but hopefully the effect would be the same.

He slid the pizza off the pizza stone and onto a large serving platter. Then opened the bottle of Chianti so it could breathe before Charlotte got home.

"Charlotte will be here soon. Do you want to stay and hang out with us?"

Piper looked up and seemed to give it a good think. But then she bit her lip and shook her head. She tucked her tablet under her arm and slid off the stool, refusing his offer to help her back to her room.

Damn, he wished he could connect with her somehow.

"Hey," Charlotte said from the doorway.

John had seriously underestimated how seeing her again would affect him. She had her hair pulled back in a casual ponytail, revealing the sharp curve of her jaw and the length of her smooth neck. Her cargo pants hugged her curves just right, and her soft, peach-toned tee shirt brought out the color in her cheeks.

"Hey, yourself," John said, resisting the urge to welcome her home with a soft, warm kiss.

Exactly the kind of urge he'd feared when Sarah had proposed this arrangement.

Her gaze slowly scanned the kitchen. John hoped she wouldn't take offense at the mess of flour and sauce and pans all over her counters. But when her gaze settled back on him, she just smiled.

"This is nice, John. The house actually feels cozy."

He knew just what she meant. Once Piper was settled in her room, he had taken a tour of the downstairs. He knew Charlotte's home was under renovation, and he wanted to know which areas were too dangerous for Piper to navigate on crutches. Thankfully the crew seemed to be focusing on Charlotte's basement this week, working to remedy some water damage.

The house was just as Charlotte had described—spacious and grand in many ways, but also cold.

Maybe it was because many of the rooms were empty, cleared of furniture in preparation for the eventual house sale. But in a way John couldn't describe, the house felt like an empty shell. As if no one had ever really lived there. It troubled him that this was where Charlotte ended her days after caring for their patients at the clinic.

John held up the pizza. "Made your favorite."

She cocked her head. "You made a pizza just for me?"

"It was the least I could do, considering Piper and I have taken over your castle."

She smiled as she looked around. Piper's homework waited on the counter…a single shoe had been kicked off by the door. "I like what you've done with the place. Speaking of Piper—where is she? I'd love to meet her."

"She's either battling aliens or role-playing in an alternative universe at the moment. I'm sure she'll join us later, when she sees the chocolate eclairs we're having for dessert."

John reached into the glass display case that was suspended over the kitchen island. He found two wine glasses among the stacks of porcelain dinnerware and poured her a glass of wine. He detected a hint of her perfume as she took the glass. Something sweet and mysterious, plus those jasmine notes that always trailed after her. For just a moment, he could imagine this as his life. Making dinner for Charlotte, with Piper safe and sound down the hall. Just like a real family.

Whoa! What on earth was he thinking? He and Piper hadn't even spent a night in Charlotte's home and he was already thinking of them as a family! He turned away from Charlotte, hoping she wouldn't see the intense emotions playing out in his heart.

"I have some good news," she said, reaching past him for plates.

Her arm brushed his as she passed, setting every hair on his arm to attention.

"I could use some good news." John busied himself with finding cutlery and napkins for dinner. He had to get these unruly emotions under control.

Charlotte added pizza slices to two plates. "The chair of pediatrics signed off on Angel's charity application. It's being forwarded to the financial services department for processing. Once we get official approval, I'll set up Angel's EKG."

That was good news indeed. But the rush of relief he should have felt was muted from the stress of his week.

Charlotte took a small bite of pizza, then closed her eyes with pleasure. "*So* delicious, John. I think this is the first homemade meal I've had since I came to Seattle."

"Seriously? You don't cook?"

"I move around too much to justify hauling around heavy kitchen mixers or a full set of saucepans. Besides, there's no better way to experience a new place than through its food." She set her glass down and crossed her arms on the counter. "I thought you'd be more excited about Angel's application. Is something wrong?"

Was something wrong? What a funny question. Six months ago, his life had been simple enough. He'd worked too much, then spent all his free time preparing *The House Call* for its next adventure. Now he was living as a guest in the house of a colleague he was incredibly attracted to, thanks to his failure to keep his niece safe, no matter how hard he'd tried.

"No, everything's fine."

Because it had to be. His life and his problems had nothing to do with Charlotte. She was a free spirit, destined to spend just a month or two in Seattle before she flew off to more exciting destinations and assignments. She didn't need to be burdened with his problems.

"I see." She drummed her nails against the counter. Then she cocked her head and smiled playfully. "Don't mind if I do."

He mimicked her head-tilt. "Don't mind if you do, what?"

"Have that second glass of wine you want to offer me."

She peered past his shoulder to the half-full bottle of Chianti he had placed out of reach.

He shook his head with chagrin. "What is it about you that makes my manners disappear?"

That was a rhetorical question, of course. He knew exactly why he acted like an angsty teen whenever she was around. Because he liked her. A lot. She was beautiful, smart, and when he wasn't acting like an idiot, they had a really cool vibe between them.

He poured her another glass of wine, then topped off his own. He kept her company while she ate a second slice of pizza and caught him up on the clinic's schedule for the upcoming week.

When she'd finished, she blew him a chef's kiss. "That was delicious, John. Thank you." She folded her napkin, pushed it aside and leaned back in her chair. "All right, Bennett… Start talking."

"About what?"

"About whatever's making you look as mopey as a hound dog, as Sarah would say."

"Do I?"

He ran a hand across his jaw, stubble chafing his palm. He'd been too busy tending to Piper to focus on himself for these past few days. Charlotte waited, both hands cupping her wine glass. Her expression was patient and attentive. For one moment John was so tempted to let down his guard. To share his worries about Piper and his fears that he would fail as her guardian. But that wasn't fair to Charlotte. Why would a free spirit like her want to get wrapped up in his problems?

"I'm probably just tired," he said, offering his best attempt at a smile.

She eyed John for a long minute, as if she was weighing the merit of his reply. Finally, she shrugged and swirled the wine in her glass. "Sorry, Bennett. I just don't buy it."

John chuckled, surprised at her response. "Don't buy what?"

"The baloney you're peddling here. I know you're upset about something."

John couldn't imagine how she was so certain.

Reading his expression, she clarified. "It's this funny thing you do with your eyebrows when you're upset. You kind of squash them together... like this."

She mimicked the look for John, pushing her eyebrows together furiously while pursing her lips at the same time. She looked like one of the angry characters in Piper's video games.

John couldn't help but laugh. "I do not look like that!"

She sat back with an amused smile. "Yeah, you kind of do. But it's okay. You're still my favorite workmate."

He shook his head as he looked down at his glass. She was teasing him, and he rather liked it. It felt good to have someone in his life who knew him well enough to tease.

She leaned forward, resting her chin on her hand. It only made her look even more enticing. "Sometimes sharing our burdens makes the load a little lighter, yes?"

Why did she have to be so beautiful? Everything about her was warm and appealing. It was almost impossible not to lean into the moment. Maybe he could allow himself the indulgence of believing, just for an hour or so, that he didn't have to bear his burdens alone.

"Piper goes back to school on Monday," he said.

"And this is a bad thing?"

"Normally, no." The truth was he was dying to get back to the clinic. "But Piper didn't have a bike accident at school. She ran away."

Cripes, it was awful saying the words out loud.

"She showed up for her first period class, so she was there for the attendance check, but then she and a friend slipped away before the next period. They rode their bikes over a mile to a local bike park, to try out some tricks they saw on social media. It was all fun and games—until Piper's bike went one way and she went the other."

He closed his eyes against the image of her flying over the handlebars to land against a concrete barrier.

"John, that's terrible. But she's all right now, right? And what about you? Are you okay?"

"No," he shot back, immediately regretting his sharp tone. "How could I let this happen?"

Charlotte's brows knitted in confusion. "I don't understand. You weren't even there. So, how could this be your fault?"

"Because it's my job to protect her! It's up to me to choose the right sitter, the right school, the right…everything! If the school failed to keep her safe, then I failed her too. Because at the end of the day I'm all she has."

And that was his fault too, but his throat and chest were so tight he could hardly speak, let alone tell Charlotte the role he'd played in Piper's new reality.

John stood abruptly and cleared their dishes. He knew he was being too rough, clashing cups against plates and making a terrible racket. But it was oddly satisfying, the way the external clatter matched his inner turmoil. He felt Charlotte watching him, but she didn't say anything. What could she say? These problems were his to bear, and he shouldn't have burdened her with them at all.

He dropped the dishes in the sink and turned the water on full blast. Soon he had a sink full of hot, soapy water. Charlotte appeared at his side and cupped his shoulder with her soft hand. He closed his eyes against the swell of emotion her touch inspired. Somehow she was slipping past his defenses into the closed-off places of his heart, surprising and jarring him at the same time.

"Look, I don't have kids, or anything, so maybe I'm out of line here. But it seems to me that you've done an amazing job of being her safe place to land after her father went to jail. She's still grieving about her father and the loss of the home she knew. What about a therapist? Someone she can talk to and sort things out?"

John fiddled with the cloth napkins now stained with pizza sauce and wine. "We've tried a half-dozen therapists. She won't talk to them. She just clams up and stares out the window."

"Maybe you haven't found the right therapist?"

"Maybe," John muttered, then set about cleaning up the mess he had made.

Charlotte joined him, silently drying dishes while he worked out his frustrations with soap and a cleaning wand. He shouldn't have unloaded on her like that. Just a few days ago he'd been insisting that they needed to stick to being work colleagues, and now he was using her as a sounding board. This wasn't what she'd wanted when she invited him and Piper to stay here, he was sure of that.

When every dish was washed and put away,

John checked his watch. "It's getting late. I'll get Piper to join us for eclairs and coffee."

"Looking forward to it!" Charlotte said.

But John didn't find Piper sprawled on the bed with her computer or her books, like he'd expected. She wasn't in the bathroom either. The bed was still made and her suitcase sat next to the dresser, still waiting to be unpacked. But her shoes and jacket were missing.

John's heart jumped into his throat. Had she run away again?

He dashed back to the main living area, hoping against hope that Piper had somehow transported herself to the living room without him noticing. His mind was working overtime. She had a broken leg, for Pete's sake— how far could she go?

Unless all that time on her computer meant she'd been talking to someone online? Someone who could pick her up and...

John shifted to emergency mode. "She's gone!" he shouted. His throat was tight with terror.

But Charlotte was gone too.

"Out here!" he heard Charlotte call. "Bring your coat!"

John dashed outside to find Charlotte sitting in an Adirondack chair, wrapped in a plaid blanket. She was watching Piper approach a scraggly cat.

Charlotte smiled warmly at John and tapped the chair next to hers.

John sank into the chair, feeling a little wobbly with relief. "So, who's this?"

"I just call him Cat. The lawyer doesn't know if he belonged to my father or not. He visits every day, but he won't come into the house."

"What's wrong with his eye?" Piper studied the cat like he was something foreign and exotic.

Now that he was adjusting to the dimmer light outdoors, John could see what Piper was talking about. It was a tabby cat. Not young, but not a senior either. It was thin enough to count its ribs, and one eye had been scarred shut.

"I'm not sure. Maybe a fight. Or an accident. Doesn't look like he had proper veterinary care, so the eye is permanently damaged."

Piper was quiet. Then she reached out to touch the skinny creature.

"Don't!" John cried.

One bite and Piper could get Cat Scratch Disease, or rabies, or an infection of her bloodstream.

Charlotte laid her hand on John's to calm him. "Put your fingers out so he can sniff. Cat will let you know if he's feeling social or not."

John would still rather shoo the cat away, but before he could say so the cat began rubbing his face all over Piper's fingers and hand.

Piper looked up with a delighted smile. "He likes me!"

"Indeed, he does," Charlotte said. "And so far you are the *only* one he likes."

"He won't let you pet him?"

"Nope. I'm only allowed to feed him, and even then he seems to think he's doing me a favor."

The tabby was going mad on Piper now, even allowing her to scratch under his chin. A distinct rumbling sound rose from the cat's skinny belly, making Piper smile wider than John had ever seen. It was good to see her happy, even if it took a down-on-his-luck cat to make it happen.

"Why doesn't he have a real name?"

"I guess because I can't keep him. Seems better for his future family to have the honor of naming him."

Piper's smile faded. "Why can't you keep him?"

"Because soon I'll sell this house and get back to my real life. It's hard to have a pet when you move around a lot."

And there it was. The reminder he needed. Charlotte was amazing as a colleague and a friend. Her generosity in sharing her home with him and Piper was more than he'd ever expected. But he couldn't lean into this. As wonderful as it was to share an evening with Charlotte, this was just a sabbatical of sorts. He had a real life too, and it couldn't include Charlotte. He was the oak tree, deeply rooted to the earth, while she was a bird that flew where it wished. Their time together would be wonderful, but short, because that was what they were made for.

Charlotte's expression had turned thoughtful. "You know, Piper, seeing how Cat seems to like you so much, maybe you can help me…"

She cast John a sideways glance that made him wonder what she was up to.

"Cat's not going to get a good home if he's dirty and unfriendly. He obviously likes you, so maybe you could help me earn his trust? Then I could take him to a veterinarian for some good medical care. And together we could help him gain some weight, brush out his coat, and learn some basic manners."

John instantly understood her plan. When the doors to someone's heart were locked up tight, like Piper's after what had happened with her father, sometimes you had to find another way in. Piper wasn't willing to talk to a therapist about her adjustment issues, but maybe she would open up to Charlotte. Especially if the goal wasn't for her to open up, but just to help a scruffy old cat who had given up on people.

Piper was somber as she considered the offer. "He needs a better name."

Charlotte's laughter was lovely and spontaneous. "Are you negotiating your terms? Okay, it's a deal. You can name the cat whatever you want if you help me get Cat ready for his new forever family."

Cat stood and arched his back, then dropped to his forearms for a deep stretch. Maybe that meant he liked the deal too.

Piper followed Cat to the edge of the yard, watching as he easily scaled the fence and disappeared.

Charlotte called out a warning for her to stay away from the dilapidated greenhouse which clearly had not been used for a decade or more, then whispered under her breath, "Maybe the best therapist for Piper has four legs and a tail?"

Maybe so. But how was Piper going to help with Cat once they moved to a short-term rental?

She wouldn't. Not only would it be awkward and uncomfortable to set up frequent visits, there was no guarantee that Cat would be in a social mood when they visited.

So if he wanted Piper to have a chance to connect with Cat, and maybe even Charlotte, he was going to have to spend just about every minute of his day in close proximity to the woman who had captivated his imagination but was strictly off-limits.

Charlotte's hand still warmed John's arm, triggering that feeling he couldn't quite name. He searched his memory bank for another time in his life when he'd felt like this, but he came up blank.

There was a sense of relief, yes—but why? And it was mixed with some emotion that made him feel warm despite the chilly night air. As if they were a team, dedicated to helping Piper. Which meant he didn't have to go it alone.

"I think you're right. Sometimes we find help where we least expect it."

John tucked her hand into his chest, then closed his eyes and let the warmth infusing his body chase the evening chill away.

Charlotte broke down the last cardboard box and stacked it with the others for the recycling bin. The clinic's supply closet was restocked, ready for the week's work. She stretched her back and hamstrings, then grabbed a bottle of cold water from the kitchen.

She still needed to finish the draft of a federal grant report by the end of the week. John hated the mandatory reporting that came with federal funding, and she kept messing up her billing codes, so they had agreed to trade their most dreaded tasks.

Charlotte thought ahead to the end of the day, when her work would be done. Her travel journal had been badly neglected since she'd come back to Seattle. The house renovations would be done in less than a month, around the same time Piper's cast should be off. It was high time for her to start researching everything the Caribbean cruise ship had to offer.

She also needed to update her blog, *GypsyMD*. She didn't have a million followers, but those who did follow her were loyal, and loved following her adventures as a traveling doctor. If she couldn't give them an exciting glimpse into her nomadic life now, she could at least give them some teasers for her forthcoming exciting travels aboard *The Eden*.

It would be a welcome distraction from the simmering tension she felt with John in the house. It was one thing to work with him at the clinic, when they were both busy and focused on their patients. Quite another to see him padding about her house barefoot and wearing fitted jogging pants low on his hips. More than once she'd had to take a cold shower after work to get her mind out of the gutter.

Charlotte found Sarah and John in the lobby. John was sorting medical supplies into piles, while Sarah filled plastic sandwich bags with handfuls of supplies. Once a month The Sunshine Clinic closed early, so John could do street call work, where he went deep into Seattle's industrial district looking for homeless teens, sharing information about the clinic and providing medical care if needed.

John noticed her. "Hey, could you hand me those flyers?"

He pointed to a table behind Charlotte. She handed him a stack of blue flyers secured with a thick rubber band.

"Fifty!" Sarah said with finality.

She scooped up handfuls of the filled sandwich bags and dropped them into an open backpack at the end of the table.

"Perfect," John said. "We'll leave half at The House of Hope and place the others at gas stations and convenience stores in the area."

He finished stuffing the backpack with clean socks and toiletry kits.

Charlotte took a closer look at the bags Sarah was holding. They were filled with travel-sized medicines and ointments, along with a toothbrush, alcohol wipes, and a business card with the clinic's address and operating hours.

"Hey, this is your cell phone number!"

She was incredulous that John would share his personal number, rather than using the clinic's answering service for emergencies.

"If a kid needs us, I want to know. Not rely on an operator to decide if their call is important enough to page me." He shrugged on his backpack. "Ready?"

From beneath the table he hoisted a second

backpack, already filled with supplies, and held the straps out to Charlotte.

She shrugged on the backpack and groaned under its weight.

"Sorry!" John chuckled. "You're carrying the bottled water."

"Thanks a lot," Charlotte mock-complained, but she was secretly glad.

The struggle of hauling water bottles all over Seattle would be a welcome distraction from her frequent thoughts about John.

They headed into the street while Sarah stayed behind to handle phone calls and walk-ins. John gave Charlotte a lanyard that identified her as medical staff. He was hauling a wheeled blue ice chest, filled with more cold water and snack packs of apples, string cheese, crackers, and peanut butter.

Their first stop was The House of Hope, where they dropped off flyers and first aid kits. The shelter was decorated for Valentine's Day, with pink and white hearts taped in the windows. Charlotte couldn't see the kitchen, but she could smell the sweet scent of fresh-baked cookies and hear teens chattering and laughing amid the clatter of dishes being washed.

The shelter director insisted they take a few cookies for the road. Charlotte's frosted sugar cookie had *Be Mine* shakily piped by a young baker's hand. John's had a chubby Valentine cherub, his bow and arrow pointing Charlotte's way.

Not that he needed any help from Cupid. Ever since John's SUV had joined her rental in the garage, her feelings of agitation and restlessness had only multiplied. She wasn't herself when he was around. She felt awkward and overly self-aware.

John was walking ahead of her now, hauling the cooler and considering their next stop. Charlotte gazed down at his backside, admiring the muscular curves that flexed the limits of his denim jeans. *Damn.* She couldn't help but remember the night they'd worked late. That passionate but fleeting kiss…the feel of her fingers kneading his thick, silken curls.

She forced her gaze back to the work at hand. These distractions weren't going to help anyone. John had made his feelings perfectly clear. He might have enjoyed that kiss as much as she had, but moving forward was not an option.

They headed deeper into Seattle, stopping at churches, gas stations and the community center to drop off flyers and first aid kits. Clerks and volunteers suggested places where they had seen teens who might need their help. Charlotte had to walk fast to keep up with John, as he seemed determined to investigate every lead before dark.

The sun edged closer to the horizon. Charlotte jiggled her pack. "I have a few water bottles left."

John rubbed his chin. "One last stop, then— the skate park. We'll pass out the rest of our supplies, then head back to the clinic."

Despite the waning sun, the skate park was in full swing. Kids gathered in big and small groups, boasting and laughing, skateboards resting under skinny arms or leaned up against the fence. John focused on two girls near a cherry tree, its branches bare for a winter rest.

The girls, wary at first, soon warmed to John's gentle curiosity. The taller girl in skinny jeans said she knew about the clinic but didn't have plans to visit anytime soon.

"Keep the card," John said, pointing to the kit. "In case you need us."

She tucked the card in her back pocket. "Okay. But you guys should check on Tommy."

The shorter girl, with chipped, bubblegum-pink nail polish, pointed to a white cargo van. "Yeah, he's pretty sick."

The van was parked at the back of the parking lot. Based on the flat rear tire and the tall weeds growing through the front fender, it seemed it hadn't been moved in a long time. The rear door was open and Charlotte could see a boy, lanky and thin, lying on his side with his back to the world.

She and John approached the van slowly, calling the boy's name. It took almost a dozen attempts before Tommy moaned and turned their way.

"Hey, Tommy." John's voice was warm and soothing. "My name is John. I'm a doctor, and so is my partner, Charlotte. Your friends are very worried about you."

The boy opened his eyes but seemed too exhausted to keep them that way. He threw an arm across his face. "Man, I am *so* tired. I've been sleeping for *days*."

Charlotte scanned the boy from head to toe, assessing his condition. Her first impression was that he was a fast-growing adolescent who needed more calories than he was getting. His sandy brown hair needed a shampoo, and his jeans were frayed at the bottom. But what really concerned her was the beads of sweat on his forehead and his too-pale skin. Tommy was a very ill boy.

"Okay if I check you out?" John asked.

But Tommy didn't answer. He had already slipped back into unconsciousness.

Charlotte fished the blood pressure meter and thermometer from her pack. She accepted a pair of latex gloves from John, then took Tommy's temperature. One hundred and one degrees. Elevated, yes, but not dangerous. Ditto for his blood pressure and heart rate.

John gently pinched the skin on the back of Tommy's hand. It stayed tented. "He's dehydrated."

Charlotte draped her stethoscope around her neck and considered the boy. Tommy's eyes, when open, were vacant and confused. He clearly needed more than fluids and rest, but his vitals were that of a relatively healthy teenager. What could be wrong?

If only she had an army of highly trained doctors and nurses, ready to run any test she wanted. Or the benefit of a full medical history delivered by a parent or guardian who was intimately familiar with his history. But out here, bent over a sick boy in a rusty van, all she had was her intuition and the equipment she could carry in a backpack to save a boy who was deteriorating before her eyes.

But she also had John.

"Let's try an orthostatic," she said.

"That's pretty old school."

"I know, but it's worth a shot."

Tommy was beyond the typical age range, but it was possible that his body retained a child's ability to hide symptoms of serious infection. If so, getting him to stand would overwhelm his defenses and reveal how sick he really was.

John helped her to get Tommy to struggle to his feet. He was so weak John had to support his full body weight while Charlotte checked his vital signs again. She frowned at the new numbers. His blood pressure had plummeted while his heart rate had soared to one hundred and fifty beats per minute.

Alarm bells rattled her core. "Sepsis," she muttered.

John's gaze darkened. They both knew that without immediate medical intervention the inflammation raging through his body could damage his internal organs to the point of death.

Charlotte reached for her cell phone to call 911, but John growled, "No time!" All traces of the easygoing Dr. J were gone.

They maneuvered the moaning boy back into the van, barely aware of the growing crowd of teens gathered around watching them, silent and somber.

Charlotte dug through the cooler for the IV bag of antibiotics and saline, while John started a large bore catheter. They worked carefully, laser-focused on starting the IV fluids that would fight off whatever systemic infection was shutting Tommy's organs down.

John held a stethoscope to Tommy's chest while Charlotte called for an ambulance. Soon she heard the high-pitched wail of a screaming siren headed their way. Tommy's breathing had slowed ever so slightly. There was even a hint of pink in his cheeks. Charlotte allowed herself a tiny sigh of relief. Tommy was still in danger, but this baby step of improvement was a relief.

The ambulance crew arrived, and John completed the handover, squeezing Tommy's hand as he was loaded into the ambulance. The teens drifted away slowly, murmuring in hushed whispers.

With the crisis behind them, Charlotte's adrenaline rush was soon replaced by a crushing fatigue. She dropped like a stone onto a rickety wood bench. John sat next to her, the bench groaning under the extra weight.

"Will we ever see him again?" She felt cold and numb as she contemplated the near tragedy.

"Probably not."

Her stomach clenched with delayed fear. "That was too close, John. We almost lost him."

To her dismay, her voice was shaking, betraying emotions she couldn't control. She didn't realize her hands were shaking too until John folded both of his around hers, buttressing them against the late-day chill that seemed to rise from the damp earth beneath their feet.

"I know."

His voice was so calm. Like he had seen this a thousand times before—which maybe he had. But how could he stand it?

"I don't get it, John. What happened? How can a boy be *that* sick with no one to care for him?"

John's jaw clenched for just a second. "I don't know, Charlotte. Asking why too often can drive you crazy. These kids are like ghosts. You see them going to school, working a part-time job, trying to fit in. They work hard to hide what they lack. Teenage bravado, maybe, or an instinct to hide weakness on the street. I don't really know."

His grasp tightened around her hands, and she looked up to see his clenched jaw.

"But I do know this. They're worth saving. Every last one of them."

John released one hand so he could trace her cheek with his finger.

"What about you, Charlotte? Are you worth saving?"

Charlotte gasped at his question. "What are you talking about? I'm nothing like Tommy! He's completely alone in the world, with no one to look out for him except us. I have…"

She trailed off. Who did she have? Who could she count on to come to her aid at any time of the day or night, no questions asked?

She had thousands of followers who loved to live vicariously through her travel blog. But they didn't know her.

Even the friends she met every year or two for an exotic vacation didn't know her all that well.

Certainly not well enough to drop everything in their life for her if she were sick or injured.

Which was by design—so that she didn't have to feel the pain of saying goodbye to someone she cared about.

But she had never asked herself why she kept saying goodbye in the first place.

"So who would be there for you if you were as sick as Tommy? Who would refuse to leave your side until you were strong enough to take care of yourself?"

"I *am* strong enough to take care of myself!" She always had been—ever since her mother had died.

That was enough to trigger the memory of that terrible night. First the policeman, who'd delivered the terrible news. He'd asked if there was anyone he could call for her, but there had been no one. It had always been just her and her mom. A tiny family of two, complete in and of themselves. But she was gone and so the social workers came.

She had only been allowed to take what would fit in the trash bag they gave her. She'd packed as if she'd be gone for just a night or two, leaving so much behind. Pictures and collected seashells. Her mother's recipe collection and Charlotte's saved art projects. Ticket stubs and favorite slippers and the soft blanket they'd snuggled under for their movie nights.

John's steady gaze was stripping her bare. All

he wanted was her truth. But she wasn't sure she knew it anymore.

She was certain of one thing. She was tired of running. She could feel it in her bones.

Because what was the worth of a life spent living like a tourist? That was what she was, essentially. What was she missing by being always on the road, never dug in? Was she happy never making a difference in anyone's life because she was always on the move, always planning her next adventure, always one step ahead of heartbreak and hurt?

Instead of a family she had a travel blog. Instead of love she had a well-worn passport.

It had been enough for a long time…when she was defining herself after her years in foster care.

But what about now?

She sighed and looked down at the hands that enveloped hers. Hands that belonged to a good man who always stayed, no matter how it might crush his heart with despair.

She checked her neck—there was no itching, no feeling of imminent danger. For the first time in a long time, maybe forever, she felt like she was right where she wanted to be.

CHAPTER SEVEN

BY THE TIME Charlotte and John got back to the clinic, it was long past dark. The clinic was locked and Sarah's car was gone. Charlotte had barely spoken after Tommy's perilous rescue and now, under the parking lot's lamps, John noted dark shadows under her eyes. He didn't press her for conversation as they unpacked the coolers and prepped for the next day.

"See you at the house," she mumbled as she rooted through her purse for her car keys.

John's stomach fluttered with alarm. Everything from her slumped shoulders to her slow gait screamed fatigue. His partner was far too tired to be behind the wheel of a car.

"Let me drive you home," he said.

"I'm fine," she countered, but it sounded like a reflex.

John paused, considering his options. Just long enough for her to unsuccessfully smother a huge yawn.

She gave him a sheepish half-smile. "Maybe you're right."

She dropped her keys into his hand and followed him to the car. John slid into the driver's seat and pressed the car's ignition button. The radio picked up Charlotte's playlist, playing an R&B song that was a soothing balm after their long day.

John turned on the car's heater, then checked his texts. Piper had gone to a friend's house after school, her first ever playdate since she had moved in with John. Living with Charlotte and finding camaraderie with a cat who didn't know where he belonged either had helped her find her bearings a bit, and helped John to see that in his desire to protect Piper he might have accidentally smothered her. If she was going to heal, he had to help Piper find her own village of friends and caring adults. And maybe a dumb cat too.

John texted the friend's mother to let her know he was on his way to pick up Piper.

She was blossoming at Charlotte's house. Sometimes John woke on his days off to find Piper's bedroom empty. Instead of the rush of alarm he'd felt that day when he'd been having pizza with Charlotte, he knew exactly where to find her. In Charlotte's kitchen, perched on the counter, helping to stir eggs or just chatting away while Charlotte made breakfast. Sometimes they both worked on the cat, brushing his fur out or showing him the joy of feather wands.

Their work seemed to be paying off. John could no longer count Cat's ribs at a glance. Cat was filling out with a steady diet of good food and extra treats.

In time, it had become natural to start their mornings in Charlotte's kitchen, with sunlight streaming through the windows while soothing music played on the speaker. Charlotte and Piper had little jokes that he didn't understand. But he liked to watch them while he pretended to read the news on his phone. Their easy camaraderie and quick laughter mixed with the music and the smell of coffee brewing and the sizzle of eggs and bacon on the stove. They were like threads in a tapestry, all woven together into something that felt warm and nurturing.

As they left the clinic, John realized he was famished. Charlotte must be too. Had they eaten lunch? He couldn't remember. But it was far too late for a restaurant, and local fast food was awful. They needed something simple, but quick. He spotted a coffee shop ahead, its interior lighting glowing amber against the dark, wet streets of Seattle, and drove in.

The aroma of fresh brewed coffee and sweet treats paired with the intense grinding and hissing of professional-grade coffee machines met him at the door. A glass display case was filled with croissants and bagels, sandwiches, fruit tarts, and a dizzying array of baked goods. John had no idea what Charlotte liked, so he chose a little of everything, then capped it off with two herbal teas.

Back in the car, Charlotte sniffed the steam escaping the takeout lid. "Mmm, chamomile," she breathed. "Perfect choice."

Just then it started to rain. Huge, fat drops that thumped on the windshield and roof of the car. He dialed the heat up two degrees and headed for their shared, temporary home.

The tea seemed to revive Charlotte. She peered into the backseat. "What smells so good?"

His best guess was the toasted buttered bagel, because the smell of it was making his stomach growl too.

She reached for the bag and the next thing he knew she was offering him half.

She groaned with pleasure at her first bite. "It's like you picked my favorite before I even knew it was my favorite!"

Was it ridiculous to feel this much pride at pleasing her? Maybe so, but he couldn't deny the shiver of pleasure that spiraled up his spine.

When they picked her up, Piper was equally pleased with the bag of goodies. She happily snacked on the chocolate chip muffin he had selected just for her and spent the trip home regaling them with stories of her adventures with her new best friend.

John guided the car out of the rain and into the garage. He silenced the engine, then checked the backseat, wondering what had happened to Piper's happy chatter. She was sleeping, curled into a tight ball, still holding her half-eaten muffin.

"Out like a light," Charlotte whispered.

"She must have had fun."

John plucked her from the backseat while Charlotte held her injured leg for support. They worked silently to tuck Piper into bed.

"Wait," Charlotte whispered. "I have something for her."

A few minutes later she was back, with a small gift bag that she gave to John.

"That's really thoughtful, but shouldn't it wait till morning?"

Charlotte shook her head with a smile. "She needs it now."

It was a nightlight in the shape of a lighthouse, its beacon providing a soft amber glow to illuminate the nooks and crannies of Piper's room.

"Ever since you and Piper moved in, I've been searching for a sailboat nightlight, to remind her of *The House Call.* But when I saw this one, I thought it was a good second choice." She looked down at the sleeping girl between them. "I like lighthouses. They can guide you back home, wherever that home might be."

They unloaded the car, and he followed her to the kitchen, where Charlotte busied herself with gathering up the takeout order and her purse.

Just when John was about to wish her goodnight, she held up the takeout bag.

"Want to join me for dinner?"

It was the exact opposite of what he should do. He liked her too much…was too keenly aware of her scent and her movements, the tiny freckle on her chin, her favorite music and how she liked her coffee.

But the stress of Tommy's rescue lingered in the knotted muscles of his shoulders and neck. It had been a close call—far too close for John's comfort. It would be nice to share the end of the day with someone who understood.

He must have hesitated a breath too long, because she looked down with a pained expression and toyed with a thread on her pants. He could hear what she didn't want to say out loud.

She didn't want to be alone.

"Of course," he said, aiming for the same casual tone. "I don't want to be alone either."

Which was a funny thing. Between Piper, the teens at the clinic, Sarah, and his colleagues at the hospital, John was rarely physically alone. But sometimes he felt like being in a crowd only amplified how isolated he felt. He was there, but not truly seen—or understood. It hadn't been until Charlotte joined the clinic that he'd had reason to question the grind of his life. Charlotte and her piercing questions had let him know she saw exactly who he was and what he had sacrificed to be what others needed him to be.

When Charlotte was close, he felt like he was more than a doctor, his brother's keeper, Mr. Responsible. She made him feel like he was a man with dreams of his own that mattered.

Charlotte set the café bag on the marble countertop and began searching for plates and cutlery.

They usually used the kitchen for their breakfast dates, but he wanted something more intimate and comfortable for tonight. He looked past the kitchen into the family room. It was smaller and seemed less formal than the great big room at the front of the house. There were pretty French doors that opened out to the lawn and the woods beyond. And a brick fireplace—though that had been painted white too. Still, this was a space he could work with.

He found a plush navy-blue comforter and a few candles in the hallway linen closet. In just a few minutes he had started a fire and lit a row of candles on the mantel. He shook out the comforter and laid it on the floor, just as Charlotte rounded the corner holding a tray laden with food.

"Voila!" John said. "Who says you can't have a picnic in the rain?"

She froze, considering the scene, and for a moment John feared he'd made a mistake. But her surprise quickly warmed into a smile.

"Lovely!" she pronounced. "I didn't think this house could be cozy, but you pulled it off."

"At least in this room." John settled on the comforter. "So, do they have any leads?"

She joined him. "Leads…?"

"The police. I imagine they must have an all-points bulletin out on your missing furniture."

She laughed, and John decided he could happily spend the rest of his life making that happen.

"No, it's all gone. I sold it—as per the plan. The last thing to go is the house." She bit into a berry tart and sighed with pleasure.

John chose a turkey sandwich from the serving tray. "When will you sell the house?"

"When we don't need it anymore."

When *we* don't need it anymore. He realized what was holding her back. "You're waiting because of me and Piper?" Guilt overshadowed the pleasure of being alone with her.

But she waved off his concern. "Don't be silly. I'm thrilled to see this house put to good use. You can stay as long as it takes for Piper to heal.

I don't start with *The Eden* until the spring, so there's plenty of time."

Her mention of her next adventure was an unwelcome reminder of the invisible clock that held power over his life. Funny how he had balked at the prospect of sharing his clinic with another doctor. Everything was so different now. It was getting easy to imagine Charlotte as his partner at work.

And now, with the firelight casting a soft glow on her hair and the curves of her face, it was getting easy to imagine her in his bed too.

"So, why do you think he left you all this— after years of…?" His hand found her knee, embraced its curve.

"Of wanting nothing to do with me?" She smiled and stretched. Her hand found its way to his, landing light as a butterfly atop the one he had clasped around her knee. "I really don't know. I imagine it's in the letter."

"What letter?"

"The letter my father left for me. It's in the kitchen, on top of the toaster. Maybe I'll read it someday. Then again, maybe not."

"You don't want to know?"

She plucked at a loose thread on the comforter, her jaw tight with tension. "If I read his letter, it feels like I'm letting him have his say. I'm not sure I want him to have that space in my head."

She took a deep breath and softened. "I don't know. Maybe in time I'll get curious. But for now, I just want to sell this monstrosity of a home so I can donate the proceeds to charity."

And get back to my real life.

He heard the words, even if she didn't say it out loud.

"So, no settling down for you, then? White picket fence, two-point-five kids, that sort of thing?"

Why on earth should his body be so coiled with tension? Her future personal plans were none of his concern. But once again his body was betraying him, revealing the disconnect between his sensible thoughts and what his heart truly wanted.

"When I was young I was rather angry about how my life had turned out. Bouncing from house to house in foster care was rough. But when I learned about locum tenens jobs, and how I could help kids anywhere in the world, I realized those foster care experiences could be turned into something positive. Not everyone can live like a nomad, with their whole life stored in a single suitcase. But thanks to those foster care years, I can."

"And being such a wanderer...does it suit you?"

The fire had warmed the room now. Its flames were casting dancing shadows on the wall. A log snapped loudly and shifted in the grate. The candles flickered in time with the steady beat of the rainstorm outside. This moment felt insulated and private, as if he had somehow managed to stop time so that the entire world had narrowed to just the two of them in the little cocoon he had created.

Maybe it was this sense of otherworldliness that made it seem so natural for him to brush an errant strand of hair from her eyes. She didn't flinch a bit. She just held his gaze, steady and thoughtful. Her chest rose and fell with each breath, her gold pendant reflecting the firelight.

"Until now," she whispered.

"Charlotte?" His heart was a thief, stealing the moment to claim its deepest desire. "Did you really forget our first kiss? That night at the clinic?"

She tilted her head, baring her delicate throat. "I thought it was a dream."

John leaned into her. Close enough that he could feel her breath as her chest rose and fell. "I think I want to renegotiate the terms of our agreement."

She closed her eyes, her soft, pink mouth waiting. "What agreement?"

"Exactly."

Charlotte felt his lip brush hers. His mouth was firm and warm, with a touch of intensity that quickened her pulse. She shifted toward him, felt his hand find her waist, his heat radiating through her thin shirt. It was gentle, this kiss, more like a gift or an offering than a runaway train of fiery passion. But Charlotte was keenly aware of everything about him. The musky sweet taste of his kiss. The scruff of his beard against her soft skin. The press of her breasts against his solid chest.

Her hand found the curve of his shoulder, followed it to the nape of his neck. Her fingers buried themselves into his hair, mapping him like he was a treasure to explore. Long-buried desires rose from deep in her core and rippled through her so that she opened to him fully, kissing him deeply. Their passions rose and she craved the feel of his bare skin. She wanted the length of his naked body pressed against hers so that there was nothing between them.

He had exposed what she wanted most. Someone who would touch her, love her, like this. Make her believe, even if it was just a dream, that she might be worthy of someone like him.

As if she had spoken aloud, he pulled her closer, tucking her into the curves of his body, and their tongues slowly danced as she wished the moment would never end.

But it did end—though not for long minutes— with Charlotte pulling away to catch her breath. She reached for her tea, needing something to soothe her parched, dry throat. But the tea did little to dampen the fire his touches had stoked.

She risked a glance at John, feeling as naked as if he had stripped every garment from her body. Their former agreement, as flimsy as it had been, was officially null and void. If they weren't co-workers committed to keeping their attraction in check, what were they?

She opened her mouth to ask, but something in John's expression stopped her. He was listening to something beyond the room.

"Piper? I'm in here."

She appeared at the door a moment later, rubbing her eyes, clearly a bit confused as to where she was. John rose to his feet and met her at the doorway.

"I had a bad dream," she said, on the verge of tears.

John swept her up for a hug and murmured comforting words. He gave Charlotte an apologetic smile as he took Piper back to her room, promising he would stay with her until she fell asleep.

Charlotte stayed behind to watch the fire slowly die. What on earth were she and John doing? He was committed to his niece and she was a mere visitor to Seattle and his clinic.

If this were just a fling, she might not feel this angsty mix of desire and apprehension.

If she had any sense at all, she'd put a firm end to whatever this was between them.

But she couldn't. Not after that kiss. John had set something loose in her that was not willing to be shut away again.

The time for good sense had come and gone. From here on out she was in uncharted territory.

CHAPTER EIGHT

"GOOD MORNING, DR. OWENS. This is Julia, with Seven Seas Cruise Line International. We emailed your employment contract two weeks ago but have not received your signed copy. Could you please complete that at your earliest convenience?"

The cruise ship human resources director left her contact information and hung up.

Charlotte deleted the message and drummed her fingernails against her desk. Her assignment as ship's doctor for a major cruise line was less than a month away. By now she should have a full itinerary planned for herself, detailing all the excursions and sights she wanted to see while she cruised the Caribbean.

She wrote herself a reminder note and pinned it to the bulletin board above her desk. This weekend. She would definitely look at that contract this weekend.

From the corner of her eye, movement caught her attention. A paper plane had landed on her desk. Its pilot followed close behind and dropped into the chair next to her.

"Guess what that is."

"The winning lottery numbers?"

John groaned. "I wish... That, my friend, is everything you never wanted to know about the hospital gala."

Charlotte unfolded the airplane. It was John's invitation to the hospital's thirty-seventh annual fundraising gala, with all funds raised going to support the hospital's outreach programs—including The Sunshine Clinic.

John looked less than pleased.

"That bad, huh?"

"Tuxes are involved."

Charlotte thrilled at the image of her scruffy colleague all packaged up in a smart tuxedo. "I think I'd be willing to pay to see that."

"You don't have to pay. Just say yes."

"To what?"

"Come with me to the gala. Be my date. You don't even need a pumpkin carriage. The hospital has negotiated a corporate rate for hotel rooms, so guests won't need to drive if they've had a drink or two."

"What about Piper?"

"Sarah's practically begged me to let her stay overnight with her. A chance for her to spend time with her 'adopted grandchild' before she moves south to be closer to her children when she retires."

So, they would be alone for the night...

Their gazes met and held a second too long. Ever since that kiss by the fireplace John had been extra careful about Piper. With her father in jail and having had two moves in one year, he was cautious about revealing their status as a couple.

Which made sense to Charlotte too. It wasn't fair to let Piper get invested in them as a couple when it was destined to end in a few weeks. So that meant, other than stolen kisses when Piper was busy or in bed, their love life was mostly a cauldron of barely repressed desire.

A night away in a hotel room sounded very good to Charlotte.

But John misread her long silence. "Of course, you'll have your own room. At my cost. My way of saying thank you for accompanying me."

That wasn't what she was worried about, but this wasn't the time or place to discuss it. Not with Sarah manning the front desk behind them and a whole waiting room full of noisy teens.

The front door flew open and crashed against the wall.

"Hey, Doc! I got a kid who needs help here!"

Charlotte felt a rush of adrenaline at seeing Angel again. Finally! She and John had been waiting weeks for her to return to the clinic. Now that her charity funding was approved, all they needed to do was get her to see the cardiologist.

But that would have to wait. Angel had a girl with her. Fourteen, maybe fifteen years old, was Charlotte's best guess. And very sick. Even from a distance Charlotte could see from her hot cheeks and glassy, unfocused gaze that she was in a lot of pain.

"I'll think about it." Charlotte said. She patted John's shoulder, then went to the girls.

"This one needs help for real," Angel said. All her swagger had disappeared and she seemed genuinely afraid for her friend.

"I can see that," Charlotte said. "Come on in."

She led them to her room and asked the girl to get on the exam table.

She took her vitals, noting her high temperature on a chart.

"What's your name, honey?" she asked as she checked the girl's lymph nodes around her neck. The swelling there indicated her immune system had been working overtime to fight off some kind of infection or virus.

"Lily," the girl whispered. She was cradling the right side of her head in one hand and looked absolutely miserable.

"Does your head hurt?"

Charlotte cataloged the possibilities. She worried Lily had meningitis, and the swelling around her brain and spinal cord was causing extreme discomfort. But a bad virus could cause nasty headaches and a fever too.

"My ear…" Lily whimpered.

Charlotte's heart squeezed with sympathy for this girl who was suffering.

"We'll get you something for the pain in just a minute," she promised as she retrieved the otoscope.

Lily was hesitant to stop guarding her ear, but Angel turned out to be an unexpected ally.

"It's okay," Angel soothed. "Dr. Owens is one of the good ones."

Charlotte blushed with pride at Angel's compliment. Earning the trust of a streetwise kid like Angel was no easy feat. She just hoped Angel would trust her referral to a cardiologist too.

Lily's ear was practically on fire with infection. The delicate tissue of her middle ear was red-hot, bulging with inflammation. Despite Lily's whimpers, Charlotte gently moved the otoscope up and down, to the left and right, exploring the extent of the infection.

"Lily, could you wait a moment? I need to consult with my partner, Dr. J."

My partner.

Two words Charlotte had never said in her adult life.

John joined her in the hallway for an impromptu consultation.

"I'm pretty sure she has mastoiditis," she told John. "I didn't think that happened outside of medical school lectures. Can you confirm?"

John followed her back to the exam room and examined Lily's ear for a second time. He sighed deeply and clicked off the otoscope.

"I'm sorry, Lily, but we can't treat this here. You have an ear infection that has spread to a hollow bone behind your ear called the mastoid bone. Now it's filled with infection, and it could rupture any minute. If that happens, the infection could get into the covering around your brain and cause meningitis."

Lily was in so much pain she didn't care what happened next so long as they didn't touch her ear again.

John called for an ambulance to transport Lily to the hospital, leaving Charlotte free to focus on Angel.

"Thanks so much for bringing her in, Angel," she said. "She really needed a friend like you."

Angel gave her a shy smile.

"I'm really glad to see you again. How have you been feeling?"

Angel bit her lip. "I still get a little dizzy sometimes."

"Well, then, I hope you'll think this is good

news. The hospital wants to pay for your EKG testing, and we have a cardiologist who can see you on short notice. In fact, she could see you today."

Charlotte hoped that wouldn't scare Angel away, but she had to ask. Lily's ear infection was just one more example of what happened when kids didn't get good medical care fast enough.

Charlotte beamed when Angel sheepishly agreed to go.

She would have loved to drive Angel to the specialist herself, but hospital rules made that impossible. Instead, she gave Angel a bus pass and directions to the hospital. She watched Angel head off for a long multi-bus trip on her own, carrying a plastic bag that Charlotte had filled with chilled water and snacks.

Free transportation
In-house EKG testing

Charlotte mentally added two more items to her running list of services she would like to add to the clinic. She didn't know why she did this, except that she kept discovering more hidden needs in this little medical center.

But that was just the beginning. She'd been there long enough to know the kids needed far more than medical care to get their lives stabilized. They needed help getting proper identification, mental health services, and a nutritionist who could address the malnutrition that afflicted nearly every kid she worked with.

Sarah interrupted her musings. "Charlotte, I don't know what to do. Piper's school is on the phone and I can't reach John."

Charlotte felt her chest tighten. "Is Piper okay?"

"She's fine…she's fine. But she's gotten herself into another scrape at school and the principal wants her to go home. John's still at the hospital with Lily. They weren't too keen about admitting one of our patients without a consult from the emergency department attending."

"When will he be back?"

"No telling, love. Hospital admissions can take—"

"Forever," Charlotte finished.

Charlotte texted John but didn't get any more of a response than Sarah had. He was probably focused on getting Lily admitted as quickly as possible.

"Page the on-call pediatrician and ask them to come in. I'm going to get Piper. Tell John if you see him first."

John had added Charlotte to the school's list of Piper's "safe persons," so the principal was able to give Charlotte a report on Piper's latest scuffle. This one had earned her a three-day suspension from school, and the principal said she would like to see John "at his earliest convenience."

That does not sound good.

Charlotte knew that Piper's future at the school was hanging on a thread.

She took Piper home and headed to the kitchen, where she kept the first aid kit.

"Let's take a look, okay?" She indicated the scrapes on Piper's arms and knuckles.

Piper shrugged and hoisted herself up to sit on the kitchen counter.

Charlotte used antibacterial soap to clean her scrapes. "What happened anyway?"

"Some girl said something I didn't like."

"If anyone at school is bullying you, your uncle will help you. You know that, right?"

Piper jutted her chin and looked away. "No one's bullying me."

"So what happened, then?"

Piper shrugged. "I just didn't like the way she looked at me."

"That's it? All this because someone looked at you funny?"

"I guess…"

Charlotte rinsed the cuts with disinfectant, then applied a thin layer of antibiotic ointment while she tried to understand this version of Piper. With Charlotte, she'd always been a sweet kid. Gentle with Cat, helpful at home. Always polite, though a bit subdued. This combative side of Piper just didn't make sense.

Charlotte used her knuckles to gently guide Piper's head up and her gaze to her own. "Hey, kid. What's happened here? Why are you in trouble all the time?"

Piper's eyes brimmed with tears. "It won't make sense."

"Try me."

Piper took a deep breath, looked out the window. "I don't mind being in trouble."

"How come?"

"Cause if I get in enough trouble, they'll have to send me to jail." Piper shifted her gaze back to Charlotte. "Then I could be with my dad."

Understanding rolled through Charlotte's body like a gentle wave. Everything—the fighting and rule-breaking, even Piper's running away from school—made sense when viewed from the limited perspective of an adolescent girl's view of the world.

Charlotte set the last Band-Aid in place. "Does your Uncle John know that's what you want?"

"No, but he never asks either."

With that, she slid off the counter, tucked Cat under her arm, and went to her room.

By the time John got home, Piper had fallen asleep, with Cat tucked in a tight ball at her feet.

Charlotte warmed up some leftovers and kept John company while he ate. She filled him in on Piper's troubles at school and what she had learned from their talk.

"Has she seen her dad since he went to jail, John?"

John's expression was pained. "I haven't wanted to do that to her. I see Michael every month, but the whole process of getting through security... the environment...it's all so bleak."

"To you and me, sure. But she needs to see him, John. And he needs to see her too."

"I know." John sighed and let his head fall back to rest on the couch.

Charlotte settled in next to him. "What are you afraid of?"

"That she'll blame me for her father being there."

Charlotte handed him a glass of wine. She studied his profile, illuminated by the cozy fire that John had started when he got home. "Why would she blame you, John?"

John exhaled in a long, low sigh. "When our mother died, she left us a little money. Michael used his to go to art school in California. I used mine as seed money for the clinic. I thought that we were all grown up, and it was safe for me to focus on my dreams. Michael came home after a year, bringing baby Piper with him."

He smiled at the memory and Charlotte could see he loved being an uncle.

"But he seemed different. Moodier, and more prone to angry outbursts. I thought it was due to his breakup with Piper's mother and that he'd get better in time."

"But he didn't?" Charlotte surmised, hoping her patient demeanor would encourage conversation.

"No, he didn't. He got a lot worse over time. I saw him and Piper as often as I could, but the clinic was just taking off and I wanted it to be a success."

He set his wine glass on the table and leaned forward, rolling his neck to release the tension stored there.

"What I didn't realize was that Michael was undiagnosed bipolar. And his wild mood swings were driving him to spend more time with people who weren't good for him. One night…" John paused to gather his thoughts. "One night he called me for help. Said he really needed to see me. But it was the night of the hospital gala, and the chair of pediatrics wanted me to represent the clinic. I was already in my tuxedo, and the mayor was going to be there. There was no way I could skip the event."

Charlotte felt dread rolling off John in waves.

It was clear he hated even thinking about that night, let alone speaking of it out loud.

"That was the night Michael was arrested. If I had just answered his call instead of letting it go to voicemail! If I had just listened more, or been a better brother, maybe I would have realized Michael had bipolar disorder! Instead, it took a prison psychiatrist who doesn't even know him to diagnose what was in front of me all along."

John rolled his head to look at her. She saw hints of the boy he'd once been in those eyes, forced to grow up too fast. He was drop-dead handsome, but that wasn't what pulled at her heart. It was the vulnerability that he was too tired to hide. She never saw this side of him at the clinic. He was too busy being strong for the teens.

She reached out to cup his face with her hand, felt his stubble rough on her palm. He laid his hand over hers, capturing her. Then brought her hand to his mouth. She could feel his warm breath as he kissed her fingers, one by one.

She waited until he seemed calm. "That's a sad story, John," she said. "And I'm sorry that happened to your family. But just because you *feel* guilty, it doesn't mean you are."

Something that looked a little like hope sparked in his eyes.

"Thank you," he said. "I just wish things could have been different."

John turned her hand, revealing her wrist so he could kiss it, then followed a path up her arm, leaving gentle kisses in his wake. She could see a tiny scar on his chin and she itched to trace it with her fingers, hear the story of its origin.

"What's the story with this necklace?" John said, thumbing the pendant lying against her chest. "I've never seen you take it off."

Her hand flew to the pendant, as if making sure it was still there. "Really? I'm sure I have."

"You haven't." He pressed her hand to his heart. "I'm very perceptive about these sorts of things."

"It was my last birthday gift from my mother." The pendant featured a moon tarot card—a reminder that in the face of uncertainty, she should trust her intuition. She moved away from him and thumbed it unconsciously…her version of a worry stone.

John said nothing but his gaze was kind and patient. She knew he was waiting for more. And if the man had the courage to share his most painful secret with her, she supposed she could do the same.

"I was thirteen when she died."

He whistled, soft and low. "That's a tough age to lose a parent, Charlotte. That kind of thing can leave some emotional scars."

She shrugged and swirled her wine glass,

watching the ruby-red liquid cling to the glass. "I suppose…if you let it."

He cocked his head. "Why did you grow up in foster care? Couldn't Social Services find your father?"

His question took her by surprise—so direct and to the point. She was tempted to evade the question, just so she wouldn't have to tell him the truth, but that didn't seem fair after he had just bared his soul.

"A couple of months ago I would have told you no. But I just recently learned that my father did indeed know that I existed and that my mother had died." She drained the last of her wine for a bit of courage. "He opted to terminate his parental rights."

John's eyebrows rose perceptibly. "Are you serious?"

When she nodded, his usual calm, tell-me-anything demeanor disappeared. He leaned forward and took her hand in his again, grasping it firmly as if he feared she might float away.

"That's awful, Charlotte. No man should ever abandon his child. You did not deserve that."

Charlotte shrugged. "It worked out okay in the end. Because of my foster care years, I've built a pretty exciting life for myself as a traveling doctor. I'd say that's a win-win."

John's eyes never left her face. "Losing your

mother as a teen and having your father's rejection send you into foster care is not a win-win, Charlotte."

She was about to come up with another quip, to lighten the moment, but his expression said *Don't.* So, she sat frozen, not knowing what to do other than sit there with the truth that she had just shared. Her father hadn't wanted her—even when she'd needed him very badly.

John didn't say a word. It was uncomfortable at first, just sitting in silence, letting the pain of that admission swirl about in her chest. She was gripped with a strong impulse to get up and get busy. Clear the table, stoke the fire, build an addition to the house... Anything other than just sit and feel the pain of abandonment.

John stroked the back of her hand with his thumb, and she took great solace in his quiet way of saying she wasn't alone. But his words were the sweetest balm of all, letting her know that he saw what she truly feared.

"There was nothing wrong with you, Charlotte." His gaze was serious, piercing. He spoke slowly, emphasizing every word. "That was all on him. It had *nothing* to do with you."

Charlotte's pulse quickened at his perception. His eyes were as intense as she had ever seen them. As sexy as she had always found him, this level of connection was a whole new level of temptation.

Which brought its own set of problems.

She didn't think she'd be able to get by with stolen kisses and furtive glances for much longer.

Not when their attraction was deepening into something that she found quite irresistible.

CHAPTER NINE

CHARLOTTE STOOD IN front of the floor-length mirror in her hotel room, fearing she might have made a mistake. When shopping for a dress for the hospital's fundraising gala, she'd thought the floor-length, off-the-shoulder black crepe gown was a sensible choice. Paired with a little purse and crystal-embellished silver high heels, she'd thought she would make an elegant but feminine statement.

And she had achieved that for sure.

With a serious side dish of sexy.

A slit in the dress ran from the hem to her hip, much higher than she remembered when she'd tried it on, and it would undoubtedly afford a generous view of her leg as she danced. The sleeveless top showed off her neck and shoulders, along with a tantalizing glimpse of cleavage.

This was a far cry from the donated cargo pants and faded tee shirt she had worn on her first day at the clinic. Maybe too far.

She loved the way the crepe whispered when

she moved, but the way it hugged and amplified every feminine curve was making her doubt herself. This dress didn't hint at exotic travel and rugged adventure. It spoke of romance and intrigue, fantasy and fascination. It felt a little dangerous, this dress. Like it could take her places she'd never gone before.

Stop, she whispered to her reflection.

This dress symbolized her new mission of pursuing the life she wanted, not just running from what she feared. And tonight she wanted to feel elegant and pretty.

She swished the dress some more, just for the fun of it, then started working on arranging her hair into a French braid updo. She felt like a princess tonight. A princess who wasn't going to wait for the king to rescue her. She was going to save herself, slay her dragons, and then claim her prize.

She was setting the last pin in place when there was a sharp knock at the door.

She strode to the door, feeling the cool air of the hotel room on her exposed leg.

"Good evening, Dr. Bennett."

She had no idea why she went all formal like that. Maybe because she was wearing formal wear. Or maybe because the man on her threshold oozed class and elegance in a tuxedo that had been perfectly tailored to his masculine, bulky build. Powerful, sophisticated, and elegant, this new version of her colleague left her speechless.

John seemed to be having trouble finding his words too, because he just stood at the threshold of her room, his mouth open, while he scanned her from head to silvery strappy toe.

"Dr. Owens. I mean, Charlotte. I think… Wow." He shook his head and tried again. "You look quite stunning, Charlotte."

An all-glass elevator was their carriage as they traveled down from Charlotte's room to the gala downstairs, affording a generous view of the hotel's lobby as they descended. Women in beautiful gowns roamed the halls and the boutique had stayed open late, offering high-end accessories and expensive jewelry. She thought she recognized one of the women as an on-call doctor who sometimes helped at the clinic.

"Oh, look. Isn't that…?"

But John wasn't paying any attention to the activity in the lobby. Instead, he was focused on the small stack of notecards in his hand. It must be the notes for his speech as he whisper-practiced the words that he hoped would inspire donors to support The Sunshine Clinic and the other outreach programs of the hospital.

The champagne reception was in full swing when they found their way to the ballroom. Waiters swooped here and there with trays full of champagne and hors d'oeuvres, while a lone pianist played smooth background music. John flagged down a waiter and took two tall flutes of champagne for himself and Charlotte.

"Come on, let me introduce you to some people," he said.

They moved from group to group, meeting the many specialists who made the hospital one of the top-rated in North America. Then they found their way to one of the round tables, where placards printed with their names marked their assigned places.

John and Charlotte took their seats. A server soon appeared, pouring ice water into their glasses and offering a basket of assorted breads and butter. Introductions revealed that they were sharing their table with a heart surgeon and her husband, a nurse practitioner who worked in cancer care, and the Pattersons, who had an entire wing of the hospital named after them for their generous donations.

"I'm sorry, dearie, what did you say your name was?" Mrs. Patterson asked, leaning in toward Charlotte. She cupped a hand around her ear, clearly hard of hearing.

"Dr. Charlotte Owens. I'm a locum pediatrician at The Sunshine Clinic for Kids."

"Oh, that's nice. How many kids do you two

have?" she asked, her fingers curved round the top of her purse.

"Oh, no!" Charlotte laughed. "We're not married."

Mrs. Patterson beamed. "Aw, you're newlyweds, then? The babies will be here soon enough."

Charlotte just smiled back. There didn't seem to be any point in correcting her again.

John leaned over and kissed her cheek, which made Mrs. Patterson beam even more.

All too soon, the chairman of the hospital board introduced John. Charlotte gave his hand a little squeeze for good luck as he headed for the stage.

John scanned his notecards one last time. This event was all about asking the community to support the hospital with generous donations. He didn't know why the chair of pediatrics had asked *him* to be the keynote speaker this year. Asking strangers to donate thousands of dollars was way outside his comfort zone. As was admitting that he couldn't do the important work of The Sunshine Clinic on his own.

But the teens needed him to be their voice.

He arranged the cards in a neat little stack, tucked them in his pocket and adjusted the microphone.

"My name is Dr. John Bennett and I really

hate asking for help. When I was young, asking for help was terrifying. I was afraid my family might be split up if anyone knew that we sometimes couldn't pay the phone bill or afford more than the basics. Now I'm a doctor, and I take care of kids who also hate asking for help. But unlike me, who at least had a family, they're alone in the world and don't know who to trust. I want to be that person for them. The one who helps them see they deserve so much more than just basic survival. That it's safe for them to dream and set goals. That they can count on us to be there. Ultimately, I want them to understand that it's not just okay to ask for help, it's their basic human right to get it. But to do that work, I have to ask for *your* help. Because I can't do it alone—no matter how much I think I want to."

John went on to describe the vision he had for The Sunshine Clinic. Expanding it into a one-stop health clinic able to address all the medical and mental health needs of teens in crisis. Finding ways to expand its reach in Seattle and beyond, so more teens could get the support they needed. He finished by telling them about Matthew and Sam and Angel, giving human faces to the dry statistics he had captured on the index cards in his pocket.

He refocused on the audience. He felt utterly drained after exposing his deepest thoughts and desires to virtual strangers. But he also felt liberated. Whatever happened next would be what it was.

He was about to leave the stage when, from the back of the room, he heard the sound of someone clapping. Soon it was followed by another person, and then another. One by one, everyone in the room rose to their feet, clapping and smiling. There were more than a few hankies out, dabbing at damp eyes.

John was mystified. It took him a full minute to realize that the standing ovation was for him.

His throat grew tight with emotions he was having a hard time containing.

He saw Charlotte standing next to Mrs. Patterson, patting her shoulder as she dabbed her eyes with a hanky. Charlotte gave him a shaky smile through her own shimmering tears as she clapped. *Well done*, she mouthed, and he suddenly felt blissfully, crazily, unbearably happy.

With the speeches done, the lights were dimmed and the on-stage curtains parted to reveal a DJ with her equipment surrounding her. She played songs that were energetic, with a strong background beat for dancing.

John offered Charlotte his hand. "Dance with me?"

For the next hour, they burned off the nervous energy of the night, dancing and spinning and singing along with the lyrics. Charlotte pulled out the pins that held her French updo in place, letting her dark waves spill down over her shoulders and driving John crazy. It felt so good to let himself go, to dance and move with Charlotte until they were both damp with exertion.

There was a slight pause, and then the first notes of a slow ballad played. Charlotte gave John a small smile, then nodded toward the table, indicating that she was ready to head back. She was probably right. This was a professional event. The two of them slow-dancing together would definitely activate the hospital's gossip network. But he was surprised at the sudden wave of resistance that washed over him. He was so tired of ignoring his heart's deepest desires.

He stopped in his tracks. "No, please stay," he said, catching her hand.

She gave him a nervous smile. "With all these people?"

"Why not?" he said, tugging her to him. "You are my wife, after all."

She hesitated for a moment, then her eyes lit up with understanding. "That's right—we're newlyweds! At least in Mrs. Patterson's mind."

"That's good enough for me."

She laughed, and then she was in his arms. John felt her hand curve over his shoulder as he claimed the small of her back. Their free hands met, their fingers intertwined, and then they were dancing to the music, their bodies in perfect sync.

As they circled the floor—first right, then left, then right again—John felt her body slowly melt into his.

She pulled away from his shoulder to look up at him. Her mouth was candy-apple-red, plump and full. An irresistible feast waiting to be devoured.

"We danced like this at our wedding reception, didn't we?" she said. Her eyes were hesitant, as if she was not sure he'd want to play the game.

He lightly traced the curve of her jaw with his finger. "We did. And we were perfect, Charlotte. As if we'd been dancing together for a thousand years."

The dance floor was more crowded now. He tucked her closer and her body became like a reed, bending and swaying with his as they smoothly moved between the other couples.

Charlotte moved so elegantly with the music. There was something very ethereal about the way she danced, as if she were a mirage that could disappear at any moment.

Please stay, he thought.

A yearning rose from deep in his heart—for what, he couldn't say, but he knew it was awfully important. His heart beat faster with the wanting of her.

Charlotte was gazing at him with a wistful

look in her eyes. She caught her bottom lip between her teeth before asking, "And our wedding night…were we perfect then too?"

His heart literally stopped for a full beat as he realized what she was asking. There was a hint of challenge in her eyes mixed with nervousness. Because it *was* a challenge—and he knew it. They had been dancing around the question of their relationship ever since they'd met. John knew their attraction was undeniable, but so was the force of the fears that repelled them when they got too close.

They moved in rhythmic circles, gazes locked, bodies melded. She matched his movements perfectly, so that he couldn't tell if he was leading or following. Everything blurred together—he and Charlotte, the past and the present, hopes and fears…

He took a deep bracing breath and stepped into the unknown, with all its wild, sweet possibilities. "Better than perfect, Charlotte. We were real."

He heard Charlotte's breath catch in her throat. He could practically feel the want humming in her body, vibrating into his. She stopped dancing for a moment, gazed at him directly, without artifice or fear. For a moment he feared he had taken the game too far and she would disappear in his arms like smoke.

But instead she raised herself on tiptoe and

whispered in his ear. A sudden hot rush of desire swept through his body like a tsunami. He nodded and led her to the edge of the dance floor. He knew they should probably say their goodbyes to coworkers and donors.

John hovered between responsibility and desire.

Oh, to hell with doing the right or proper thing. All he wanted was Charlotte.

He grabbed Charlotte's hand and led her out of the ballroom, letting his heart guide the way.

CHAPTER TEN

MERCIFULLY, THEY HAD the elevator to themselves. John punched the button for their floor. For a moment they stood side by side, shoulder to shoulder, watching the numbers climb on the indicator. Soft music played in the background—something kind of jaunty. The entire scene was surreal, and out of sync with the urgent, pressing need she felt deep in her belly.

Neither reached for the other's hand or stole a kiss. Which was good, she thought, because just one touch would be like dropping a match on a pile of dry kindling. It wouldn't surprise her if they both went up in flames.

At last, there was a soft *ding*, signaling their floor, and the elevator doors slid open. Then John grabbed her hand and led her down the hallway to his room. With one quick swipe of his key card, the door swung open and John pulled her across the threshold.

Finally, they were alone.

As soon as the door clicked shut, John's hands

found her waist and guided her backwards, until her back was pressed up against the door. His mouth, hard and needy, found hers, shocking her breath into silence. Her body instantly responded to his. Her mouth opened to him, tasting a hint of whiskey on his lips and beneath that, the taste of him. Wild and masculine, thrilling and real. It was almost too much, all these sensations at once, and she whimpered against his mouth, needing more.

Her hands moved of their own accord, traveling the length of his arms to the breadth of his shoulders, the strong muscles of his back. But that wasn't enough—not nearly enough—and she tugged at his shirt, freeing it so she could slide her hands beneath to explore the warm, firm flesh of his belly and back.

John groaned against her lips, his breath jagged and harsh. "I've wanted to make love to you since the day you walked into my clinic."

Charlotte took a ragged breath. "Really? Because I thought you hated me."

John nipped her bottom lip, making her gasp with the shock of it, then followed with light kisses and nibbles that made a shiver of pleasure race up her spine.

"None of that is important now. Only this. Only us."

He braced both of his arms on the wall, creating a cocoon just for them, then moved his mouth over hers. She closed her eyes and let him take her deeper, until all she could see and sense was him, all around her.

She opened her eyes to find his gaze, steady and strong. He encircled one of her wrists and guided her to the sleeping area. She followed him to the foot of the king-sized bed that dominated the room. He kissed her again, this time gently, with great deliberation.

"I want to take this slow, Charlotte. I've waited so long to touch you. I need to know you, see you... I don't know if that makes sense, but..." He trailed off as he bent to kiss her again, his hands reverent as they cupped her face.

So, this was what it felt like to be cherished. To have someone make you feel like you were the most important person in the world. It felt good to be seen, but also vaguely dangerous. She stood on tiptoe, her hands on John's as they framed her face, as if he were her only chance of surviving the raging rivers of doubt that threatened to drown her.

And then he was undressing her. Slowly spinning her till her back was to him, finding the zipper cleverly hidden in the side seam of her dress. There was a sharp, hissing sound, then her dress fell in a crumpled heap at her feet. The cool air of the room rushed over her body, tensing her nipples and sending goosebumps down her back.

John's mouth found her flesh...the graceful curve where her shoulder met her neck. His mouth was warm...so warm compared to the cool room. His fingertips stroked the delicate flesh over the curve of her breasts, teasing the place just above her lacy strapless bra. It made her shiver with pleasure again.

"Look at us, Charlotte," John said, his voice husky. "We're perfect."

There was a mirror across from the bed. There she was, nearly naked and wrapped in John's arms. They fit together so perfectly, her head to his shoulder, his strength to her grace. She felt the symmetry of them, and it was so tempting to lean into him and this image, believing it would be enough to sustain them.

She turned away from the mirror, offering her profile. "The light... Can we turn it off, please?"

Not because she was ashamed, but because she wanted to block out the entire world so that all she could feel and taste was John.

He switched off the table lamp, then opened the heavy draperies so the soft glow of Seattle's nightlife was their only illumination.

Then he was back, pulling her to him, and she had her chance to even the playing field. She quickly unbuttoned his shirt, sliding her hands

up and over his shoulders, letting the shirt slide
from his back to finally reveal the strength she'd
lusted for these last long months. He was as beautiful a man as she'd ever seen, his muscles full
and firm, his belly taut with tension.

He guided her to the bed, following her down
till they lay together. He continued his slow, de-
liberate exploration, his tongue finding the soft
flesh curving up from her bra, driving her crazy
with little licks and nibbles. She arched her back,
silently begging for more, and he obliged, un-
clasping her bra and then flinging that useless
garment across the room. It made her laugh a little, his wanton playfulness, but when his mouth
found her breast and began a careful exploration
of her hidden pleasure points she couldn't laugh
anymore. She could barely think.

Had she ever been loved like this before? Definitely not. It was like he was creating her with
every touch, every kiss, every stroke of his fingertips. Finding everything good and tender she'd
kept hidden away and sculpting it out of the raw
material that was her life. She felt found, and
she knew it was because John was the first to
ever look.

She moaned as his thumb found her nipple
and teased even more pleasure from her already
heated body. Such a flood of sensations—the
roughness of his fingers, the softness of his

tongue, the solid weight of his body on hers, the beat of their hearts together... The air seemed to crackle with electricity as he hooked her lace panties with his finger and slid them off her legs. Then his hands were everywhere, exploring, finding, teasing, setting off a deep ache that started in her core and rolled out in gentle waves to every inch of her body.

He strummed her desire ever higher, till she was fisting the sheets beneath her, arching toward a release that seemed tantalizingly out of reach.

"John...!" she cried out, and she didn't know if she was begging for mercy or begging for more. "More..." she panted into the night, her skin slick with sweat.

More sensation, more pleasure, more touch and more tingles, and more long, slow, wet kisses that wiped her memory clean.

I want more, she thought.

So much more that all her doubts and fears were overcome by the raging desire she felt for him. But she couldn't say all the things in her heart. All she could do was call his name.

And then he was there, as if he had read every thought in her head, stretching the full length of his body with hers, the weight of him so reassuring in the midst of this storm that was sweeping through her, threatening to sweep her out to sea. She grasped tight to his body, finding refuge and calm there in his steady heartbeat and patient hands.

More…

John eased her onto her back. She could feel the heat of his body under her hands, hear his jagged breath against her ear. Proof that he wanted her as much as she wanted him, and it only made her crazier.

"Please…" she whispered against his kiss, and she couldn't stop herself from grinding against him, which made him growl with need.

She hooked one leg over his, felt his body shift under hers as he reached across the bed. She heard a drawer open, then the rip of foil, before his weight was fully on her again. With the moonlight bathing their bodies in a luminous glow, he found her, and she arched to meet him. The sensations that followed were so sublime Charlotte felt utterly incapable of speech or thought. Gentle and slow, he rocked her into the night. Every sigh took her home, back to a place and time when she'd felt loved and protected.

He gathered her close and rocked her until her mind was quiet and her heart full. So full she feared it would explode into a thousand points of brilliant light. And when the warm feelings in her body heated to their inevitable flashpoint, it was his body she clung to. Every shuddering wave wiped her slate clean, leaving her raw and exposed, defenseless in his arms. He cried out her name soon after. She opened her eyes and found his gaze, deep and intense, his pupils dark with pleasure.

Later, when their hearts had slowed to a normal rhythm, he spread the comforter over both of them and tucked her into the curve of his body. She listened as his breaths grew long and deep. It was tempting to let the rise and fall of his chest soothe her to sleep...

But this wasn't her room. She didn't belong there—not all night. Somehow falling asleep in his arms seemed too intimate despite their intense sexual encounter.

The digital clock marked another minute's passing.

One more minute. I'll leave when the clock is at the half-hour.

Sixty seconds later, she swore she'd leave when five minutes had passed.

But it was many minutes later when she sighed, knowing she couldn't linger in John's warm bed any longer.

He was surely deep in sleep by now.

It was time for her to go.

As if reading her mind, John tightened his arm around her, pressing her against his chest.

"Just stay," he whispered against her hair. "All you have to do is stay."

Charlotte's body went still, but her mind was running wild. It was so tempting to stay there, curled up against John. His body was warm and she could smell his uniquely masculine scent on his skin and her pillow.

"Just stay" was closing her eyes and drifting into sleep, safe and peaceful in John's arms.

"Just stay" was sharing coffee with him the next morning, planning their next date and sending sexy text messages between patients.

"Just stay" was having a future, adopting a puppy, spending their weekends painting the living room.

But *"just stay"* could also be police officers and stolen futures and having everything she knew and counted on wiped out in a split second. There was no way she could have love without accepting the risk of losing it forever.

Her body remained rigid as her mind battled furiously with itself. Want versus need…hope against fear.

The room's heater clicked on. Beyond the door she could hear a faint peal of laughter as other hotel guests found their way back to their rooms.

He doesn't mean forever. Just for tonight.

She could do this… just for tonight. She let herself slowly relax into John, melting into the warm cocoon he had created for her. And as the sun's first rays cast a faint, pink glow in their room she finally closed her eyes and drifted into sleep.

A week later found John in an exceedingly good mood. He'd come to work late, on account of taking Piper to the doctor to have her cast removed. She'd lost a little muscle tone after weeks of resting her leg, but that didn't stop her from jumping out of his SUV and skipping her way into school.

John's gait was positively jaunty as he crossed the waiting room. "Morning, Sarah," he said, swinging his backpack up to land on the reception counter. "What have I missed?"

"Not much," Sarah said. "Charlotte seems to have things under control this morning. Now, what's happened to put you in such a good mood? You look like the cat who's just eaten the canary."

"Which would not be good news for the canary, now, would it?" John said, his body pulsing with anticipation.

After weeks of consideration, he'd finally made a grand decision. There was no point in trying to hide it from Sarah. She was the eyes and ears of the place, able to ferret out anything out of the ordinary.

John opened his backpack and carefully withdrew the forms he'd spent the previous night working on. He handed them over to Sarah and waited for her response.

She popped her bifocals on the end of her nose and perused the documents, then handed them back. "It's about time, if you ask me."

He should have known better than to expect flattery or compliments from Sarah. She was old-school about that sort of thing, believing that excessive praise made a person go soft.

Still, he had thought she would be a little more excited, considering how often she had harped at him to add a second doctor to the clinic.

"It's not official, of course," he cautioned, tapping the forms into a tidy stack. "I need to talk to Charlotte first, before I submit this to Human Resources. I don't want just any doctor to work here on a permanent basis. So if Charlotte's not interested in staying long-term, then these forms will wind up in the trash."

It felt like a long shot—maybe the longest shot he'd ever taken. But after the night they'd spent together after the gala, he couldn't imagine living life as if everything was the same. These past few weeks of living with Charlotte and Cat had made him realize that maybe all his protectiveness over Piper was a mistake. All this time he had thought that he needed to ignore his growing feelings for Charlotte, so that Piper would be safe. But Piper was healing much faster now that they lived with Charlotte. Maybe, he thought, his job wasn't to protect her from anything that might hurt her. Maybe his job was to help her find a tribe of friends and family who would pick her up if she took a fall.

Sarah crossed her fingers for good luck for him as she reached to take a call. "Oh, one more thing," she said. "Your first patients of the day are waiting in your exam room."

John nodded and headed to the workstation he shared with Charlotte. Soon he'd be able to trade the old wood door for a real built-in office area. He had gathered all the supplies and just needed to carve out some time on the weekend to get the work done.

Still whistling, he carried on preparing for the day. He stopped by the coffee station first, then reviewed the day's cases.

He was just about to set off for his exam room when he noticed a bright pink note pinned to Charlotte's bulletin board.

Return cruise ship contract ASAP!

It was written in Charlotte's neat script. There were about fifty exclamation marks for emphasis.

He stopped whistling mid-note and his heart took a nosedive toward his stomach. He plucked the note from the board and examined both sides, though he had no idea what he expected to see.

So, she was still excited about working on the cruise ship. She hadn't spoken of it in so long, he'd thought maybe she was losing interest in the prospect. An assumption on his part and apparently an incorrect one at that.

He put the note back and slumped in his chair to recover. Was everything just the same for her, then? Their night at the hotel had meant nothing?

Not that she owed him anything after their shared night together. They were both grown adults, free to spend their nights where they wished. But for John, going back to the status quo was not going to be easy. He was falling for her, pure and simple. And now that he had seen how well Piper was doing with Charlotte in their lives, his fear that falling for Charlotte might hurt Piper was losing its grip on him.

He sighed and scrubbed his face with his hands. He had patients waiting. He couldn't mope here like a lovestruck teenager, hoping for a different outcome if he waited long enough.

He looked at the forms he had so meticulously completed the night before, asking the hospital to make Charlotte's job permanent.

Should he even ask her if she wanted to stay? Or were the fifty exclamation marks on that note all the answer he needed?

He contemplated that for a long minute—then dropped the forms in the trash can next to his desk.

CHAPTER ELEVEN

JOHN WAS IN LOVE.

She was beautiful and funny and had the cutest one-toothed smile he'd ever seen.

Babies weren't John's usual patient demographic, but this particular baby was snuggled in her big sister's arms. Rosa was seventeen years old and had brought baby Anna to the clinic because she was worried about her.

"She does this strange eyelid fluttering thing," Rosa said, her brow furrowed with worry. "It used to only happen when we were outside, on sunny days. But now it happens a lot inside too, especially when she's first waking up in the morning. I've rinsed her eyes and tried some of those eye drops made for babies from the drugstore. But nothing is helping."

John gently took the baby from Rosa. His heart went out to the girl. She looked as nervous and worried as any mother would. Speaking of mothers—where was Anna and Rosa's mom? That was always a tricky question, and one he'd have to approach carefully.

John lay Anna on the table and started with a basic exam. The baby girl was in excellent health. Her cocoa-brown skin was smooth and nourished, and her plump, round belly said she was getting plenty of calories every day. He noted her tiny clean white socks and the warm yellow sweater over her jumper. Someone was taking very good care of Anna.

"Sorry, Miss Anna, but I have to shine this bright light in your eyes," John crooned to the baby.

Anna flailed her arms wildly and blew a raspberry kiss, which John took as her tacit approval. Shining his ophthalmoscope in each of her chocolate-brown eyes, he determined that her basic brain function was fine and she didn't show any signs of neurological disease. The eyes themselves were fine too, without evidence of injury or disease.

But during the exam Anna had had several short episodes of her eyes rolling upward, paired with rapid-fire eyelid flutters. Each episode lasted just a second or two and didn't seem to bother Anna in the slightest.

"Does Anna ever seem spaced out to you? Like she's daydreaming and you can't get her attention?"

Rosa nodded. "Yeah. Sometimes when I'm feeding her she'll just stare off in the distance for a little bit, like she's thinking about something. Is that important?"

"It could be." John finished the exam and passed Anna back to Rosa for snuggles. Anna giggled wildly when she saw her sister, clapping her chubby hands with delight.

"Silly girl," Rosa said, giving her sister a gentle nose-bop with her finger. "I never left you!"

And you never would, John thought, instinctively knowing that for some reason Rosa had stepped in as Anna's mother and was doing the best she could with only the knowledge and resources she had as a teenager.

"So, what do you think is wrong?" Rosa asked.

Baby Anna began fussing in Rosa's arms. The long wait to see John had surely extended into her lunchtime. Rosa opened her backpack with one hand and tugged out a small cooler where a chilled bottle waited. She shook it to mix the formula, then offered it to Anna, who greedily sucked at the nipple.

John made some notes in the baby's brand-new client record before focusing on Rosa. "There's a couple of possibilities. Your sister's eye-blinking could be a sign of a behavioral tic. Most kids outgrow those in a year or less. But if not, she could have a condition of the nervous system called

Tourette Syndrome. But the fact that your sister also had periods of spacing out makes me suspicious that she's having seizures. Those spacing out spells could be absence seizures, which are like brief electrical storms in the brain that impair your sister's consciousness for anywhere from ten to forty-five seconds. The blinkies might only be eyelid myoclonia, a small seizure that doesn't impair her in any way, but all that seizure activity is not good for her brain."

Rosa was wide-eyed now, and clearly afraid. "Is she going to be okay?"

"I think her prognosis is excellent. But we need to get those seizures under control—and that means she needs to see a neurologist for testing and treatment."

Rosa's expression fell. "Oh, I don't think my family has the money for anything like that, Dr. J."

John closed his laptop and rolled a stool over so he could meet her eye to eye. "Well, let's talk about that, Rosa. And then let's talk about you."

A half-hour later John walked Rosa to the reception area and asked Sarah to set up a neurology appointment for Anna. The baby was asleep now, her dark lashes like fringes on her tiny, plump cheeks.

"And let's reach out to the hospital's Social Services, too," John told Sarah. "I'd like a social worker to contact Rosa regarding subsidized childcare options for Anna." He turned to Anna. "No more skipping school to take care of your sister, okay?"

Rosa's eyes were shiny with misty unshed tears. "Thank you so much, Dr. J. I don't know what we would have done if you weren't here."

John squeezed her elbow. "That's what we're here for."

John returned to his desk to type up the notes from the appointment. Seeing Rosa had triggered so many memories for him. He was glad he could be there for her, but it brought back memories of all his lost years. How much he had given up to try and protect his brother as best he could.

He thought of Rosa and the worry that had etched her young face. Would she blame herself for Anna's seizures? When in fact the culprit would be a rogue gene, either inherited or mutated, that had set the path in place before Anna was even born.

There wasn't anything Rosa could do to change her sister's fate. Was it possible that there wasn't anything John could have done to change his brother's fate either? Maybe Michael, like Piper, needed more than just John in his life, trying to shoulder all the burdens on his own.

Maybe he needed more in his life too. More love, more connection, more community, more support. Certainly the last few months with Charlotte had opened his heart to magical new possibilities. Thanks to her, he had been able to speak from the heart at the gala about the work they did at the clinic, garnering historic levels of donations for The Sunshine Clinic. Thanks to her, Piper's laptop sat ignored for much of the day while she played with Cat or invited a friend over for manicures and "girl talk"—whatever that was.

Was he really going to let all that walk out of his life without a fight?

The papers he'd discarded before seeing Rosa were still in the trash. He pulled them out, smoothed the corners with the palm of his hand. His heart wavered. This was a crazy idea. Did he seriously think that *GypsyMD* would want to trade her life of exotic travel and adventure for a grounded life in Seattle with him and Piper?

But he couldn't forget how it had felt to hold Charlotte in his arms that night at the hotel. To feel the struggle in her body for so many long minutes when he'd asked her to stay. He'd feared she might just flip the covers back and leave anyway. But though she'd never said a word, he'd felt the answer in her body as she'd finally softened against his chest. It had stirred his protective side, knowing that she was choosing to trust him, and he'd wanted to be worthy of that trust that night and for all the nights ahead.

That was the part of him that knew he had to ask Charlotte to stay—even if it ended in rejection. Because he deserved to have this chance. And so did she.

John slid the paperwork back inside his backpack. He would ask Charlotte tonight, after Piper went to bed, if she would consider staying in Seattle permanently.

But, drat, it was Thursday—the day he played basketball with the teens at the community center after work. He rarely missed these games. The kids had come to count on him being there every Thursday—it was a sort of unofficial office hour, when they could ask questions or check him out in a more relaxed setting.

Trust was so important in his work with these teens. Making those games every Thursday was one of the ways he earned that trust.

Okay, tomorrow, then. He'd take the paperwork home but wait until the next day to ask Charlotte to consider staying in Seattle.

Charlotte's pink note fluttered when the heat pump clicked on. It felt like a taunt. Was he sure he had until tomorrow? This note was pinned to her bulletin board to make sure she didn't forget. That meant she was going to sign that contract soon.

But if it was still taped there, she hadn't signed it yet. He still had a chance.

Enough contemplating, it was time for action.

He borrowed her notepad to write her another note.

You are cordially invited for a sunset cruise aboard The House Call. Dress is resort casual. Dinner will be served. Don't be late!

He taped that note on top of hers, to make sure she noticed it first. Then added fifty-one exclamation points for good measure.

Mickey's Café and Tiki Bar was a harborside restaurant located at the marina where John docked *The House Call*. He and Piper were frequent visitors. Piper loved the strawberry milkshakes and John loved the breathtaking views of the harbor, where he and Piper would watch various water vessels come and go. Making up outlandish stories about the people aboard and their adventures was their favorite game.

But tonight it was just him and Charlotte. He had asked Sarah if she would mind keeping Piper at her place overnight again, so he and Charlotte could sail alone.

He could feel the cold bottle of champagne he had stored in his backpack pressing against his spine. The paperwork he needed to submit to make Charlotte's position at the clinic permanent was safely stored in a different pocket. With any luck, he'd be able to pop the champagne later, to celebrate the start of a new adventure for both of them.

But first dinner. John ordered several sandwiches and side dishes as part of the café's signature "picnic to go" special, which they offered to their seafaring customers. Everything was packed into an adorable wicker picnic basket which, it was understood, customers would return to the restaurant on their way out of the marina.

John watched Charlotte as they headed toward the dock where his boat waited. With her hair down and the breeze rustling its loose, dark waves, she was truly stunning tonight.

Moose, the marina cat, was serving his self-appointed role as sentry. He was perched on a post, big, fluffy and regal. Local lore said that petting Moose before a trip would keep sailors and boats safe at sea. Charlotte obliged with a long session of ear-rubs.

John and Charlotte held hands as they followed the walkway to John's boat. It was six-thirty—half an hour past the time he usually went to the community center. Some of the regulars would be there by now, warming up and trading friendly taunts for the game ahead. More teens would trickle in over the next half-hour, greeting each other with hearty jests or tentative smiles. John knew he was the glue that held the whole evening together, helping shy kids find their place on the team and giving the strongest players a good workout.

Charlotte put her hand on his arm. "You good?"

He was doing it again—ruminating on all the people he wanted to save instead of just being with his people.

Tonight was about him and Charlotte. And Piper too, even though she wasn't there.

Charlotte spun so that she was facing him, blocking his path. "We don't have to do this, you know."

"What are you talking about?"

"Sailing. I'd love to go, but I have a feeling you'd feel better if you were at the community center."

He started to protest but realized it was pointless. Charlotte could read him like a book. "How did you know?"

"It's this funny thing you do with your face when you're worried. Want me to demonstrate?"

He laughed, remembering her demonstration of his scowling face. "No, thanks. I'm good."

John contemplated the possibility of making it to the community center to check on the teens and then getting back in time for a quick sail around the bay. He couldn't deny the nagging feeling that he was letting the teens down.

He shook off these familiar demons. He loved those weekly basketball games, but that didn't mean he should be there every single week. If he was going to build a bigger life for him and Piper, and eventually his brother, he needed to stop carrying the weight of the world on his shoulders all the time.

He gave Charlotte's hand a little shake. "Come here."

He pulled her in close and circled his arm around her waist. He could feel her smooth, warm skin through her shirt. He nuzzled her neck, deeply inhaling the sweet scent of Charlotte mixed with jasmine and the briny scent of the sea. All his favorite things mixed together in one intoxicating fragrance.

"This is the only place I want to be." He pulled back so he could see her eyes. "Okay?"

"Okay," she said, leaning into him until her forehead rested against his chest.

He stroked the back of her neck for a moment, feeling a new warmth take root in his heart and expand to fill his entire body. It chased away the guilt and fear, so that all that was left was a profound gratitude that of all the clinics in all the world, this gorgeous woman had found her way to The Sunshine Clinic.

"All right," he said, placing his knuckles under her chin so he could guide her gaze to his. "Are you ready to learn the ropes, so to speak?"

"Sure!" She laughed. "I've had a lot of travel

adventures in my life, but this will be my first time sailing."

They boarded *The House Call* and he showed her how to prepare the ropes for their voyage. Then he used the onboard motor to navigate out of the marina and into the harbor.

If he had more time, he'd take her far beyond the harbor. Past the sea lions basking on buoys and the seawall that protected the shoreline from storm surge flooding. Past the sailboats and houseboats and the seaside mansions. And past the fishing trawlers, their nets heavy with catch. He'd take her out to the Puget Sound where, if the winds were favorable, he would shut off the engine and hoist the sails and harness the power of nature to explore the islands and ports off the coastline of Seattle.

But there was little wind, so Charlotte's first sailing lesson couldn't include hoisting a sail. She accepted the consolation prize of navigating via the onboard motor while John set out their picnic dinner from Mickey's Café. With their plates full, and the boat floating far from the shoreline, they sat on the deck to eat dinner, their legs dangling over the water.

John didn't think this moment could be any more perfect. There was the feel of Charlotte's hip and shoulder against his, the distant lights of other ships in the harbor reflecting off the water, and the very light breeze that rippled the water and made Charlotte shiver in the night. All the things he'd always wanted…all in one place. There was only one thing that would make this night more perfect.

He was about to reach for his backpack, with its contract and champagne, when Charlotte glanced up at him, her shoulder pressed to his. Their gazes met and something in her eyes made his pulse quicken. There was a sultry glint to her eyes that made it too easy to imagine her naked in his berth, stretched out on the navy-blue comforter, her hair wild and tousled against the pillow.

Oh, what he would give to have the length of her gorgeous naked body pressed against his in the same bed where he had spent so many lonely nights. He could imagine it all quite perfectly—and suddenly it was all he wanted.

He raised his fingers to stroke her cheek delicately, as if she were a very fine statue meant to be kept safe behind velvet ropes. He felt that way sometimes…that she was not really for him. Then he dropped his head to kiss her, deliberately and carefully, with great reverence.

Her lips were warm against the cold night. The soft meeting of their mouths made his soul sigh with pleasure. How could he ever doubt that she was for him? They fit together too perfectly and understood each other too well. Even their jagged edges were like the pieces of a puzzle, fitting together to make sense out of the fragments of their past.

Charlotte scooted closer to him, eventually working her way into his lap. Now she was everywhere…in his arms…deepening the kiss… asking for more. And he wanted to give her everything he had—tonight and all the nights after. His mouth became hungry and hot. He wanted to somehow pull her into his very soul. Charlotte was here, in his arms, filling all the empty places in his heart and soul.

I believe in this. I believe in us. I believe in forever.

"John…" she whispered against his ear.

Her hands had burrowed their way beyond his coat, under his shirt, and were now stroking his skin, taking his temperature higher. He knew what she was asking of him and he wished he could figure out a way to hoist both of them up from where they sat so he wouldn't have to let her go.

"Mm-hmm…" he replied.

It was all he could manage. Because Charlotte was kissing him everywhere now, and it felt so good to be loved this much. He believed that was what this could be. Love—pure and simple.

"Make love to me again…" she breathed, stirring all those lovely memories of their night at the hotel, when she had thrilled him just by asking for what she wanted.

Oh, he should do that. They should make love tonight, and then in the morning, and probably midday tomorrow for good measure.

He whispered against her lips. "Charlotte?"

"Mm-hmm…?"

He stopped her gently, pressing his fingertips against her chest with just the tiniest bit of pressure.

She broke away, but her eyes were hazy and unfocused with desire. "Hmm…?"

He traced his thumb against her bottom lip, willing himself to propose the idea of her staying long-term. But she was doing something with her fingers, tucking them into the waistband of his pants, finding the warm, hidden skin there with her sea-cooled fingers. It made him burn all over for her, and to wish for a better space to continue their explorations.

"Hold that thought," he said—then crushed her mouth with his. He felt like a starved man who would never get his fill.

Somehow they struggled to their feet without breaking their kiss. Charlotte wrapped herself around him, matching his hungry kisses with her own before leading him downstairs to his berth.

Then she jumped on the bed and landed on

her knees. And she laughed and laughed, telling him to, "Get in here, slowpoke!" She pulled her sweater off in one fluid motion, revealing her luscious curves and the sweet tease of her white lace bra.

He unbuttoned his shirt as fast as he could, but the last button was stubborn. He had no choice but to pull his shirt apart with one ferocious yank, sending the button flying across the room to land with a soft *plink*. Her eyes widened with delight as she moved aside to make room for him in the berth.

But before he could join her there was a ferocious buzzing in his back pocket—the insistent chime of a five-alarm fire bell. It was the distinctive tone he had chosen for calls from the hospital.

Charlotte froze on the bed. Their gazes met and locked. They both knew this wasn't any routine call from the hospital. Not this late on a weeknight.

He answered it. "This is Dr. Bennett."

He listened for many long minutes, asked routine questions about the patient's status. Eventually he turned away from Charlotte, so she wouldn't see what this call was doing to him.

"Thanks for calling. I'm on my way."

John disconnected the call and paused, taking one last minute for himself. One last minute of feeling loved and hopeful about his future. One last minute of living in a watercolor dreamworld where he had a vibrant, if hazy, future with Charlotte.

"What is it, John? What's wrong?"

He darkened the phone before sliding it into his pocket. He felt the mask of Dr. J slipping back into place.

"We have to head back."

"Why?" She held her sweater to her chest. "What's wrong? Is it Piper?"

John made the adjustments that would fire the engine back into life. He didn't want to talk. He just wanted to get moving…get back to work. It seemed to be the only thing the universe was willing to trust him with.

"John?" She was more insistent now, sensing the magnitude of the change in their tiny space.

"It's Angel. She went to the community center looking for me because she was feeling very sick."

"Is she okay?" Charlotte slipped her sweater back on.

"I don't know. She collapsed at the center and was rushed to the emergency room."

CHAPTER TWELVE

THE HOSPITAL'S WAITING room was filled with teens that Charlotte recognized from The Sunshine Clinic. She wanted to go with John to get an update on Angel's status, but seeing the stress and worry on these young faces, she knew she needed to stay with them.

Unlike on most of her temporary assignments, where she was the outsider looking in, the teens here had adopted her as part of their ever-shifting, highly flexible family unit. Not a family like any she had seen in movies or on television, but a family all the same.

Maybe that was why she hadn't responded to The Eden yet. The beauty and adventure of the Caribbean still called to her, but she felt a strange and utterly unfamiliar pull to stay in Seattle. She was falling for John—she knew that—and for his precocious, lovable niece. But there was more holding her in Seattle. Forces she couldn't understand, but which made it impossible for her to just board The Eden and leave it behind.

She didn't know exactly what she would do, but she knew she needed to call the cruise ship's human resources department and ask for an extension before signing her contract. It would give her more time to think and decide what she wanted to do.

Now, looking at the pale, strained expressions of the teens who had witnessed Angel's collapse, she finally understood why she felt pulled to stay. She was needed here. Piper, and the teens, and even that silly Cat, all needed her.

The only person she wasn't sure about was John. He was so self-sufficient…so insistent on doing things his way and on his own. Would he welcome her decision to stay in Seattle? Or was their love affair nothing more to him than a fling with a doctor he was sure would leave?

But she pushed those thoughts to the back of her mind as the teens told her what they had seen—how Angel had gone to the community center, pale and confused, looking for John. How she'd left and some of the teens had followed her, sensing something was wrong, and how they'd found her in the parking lot, unconscious and cold.

"It was so scary," one of the girls said. She had her arms wrapped around herself, rocking back and forth.

"Where was Dr. J anyway?" one of the boys

demanded. "He's always at our Thursday night games!"

John returned to the waiting room and the teens gathered around him for news and information. He did his best to get them caught up on Angel's status, assuring them that Angel was going to be okay.

He caught eyes with Charlotte and nodded toward the nurses' station.

"I'll be back in a second, kids. Let me just get Dr. Owens caught up."

Charlotte followed John to a quiet alcove near the nurses' station.

"The EMTs said when they found Angel she was unconscious but breathing on her own. Other than her fast heart rate, her other vital signs were good. She regained consciousness on the way to the ER, but complained of dizziness and a small headache. The ED attending wants to keep her for a few hours for observation. But if she remains medically stable, they plan to release her by morning."

Charlotte grabbed his arm. "We can't let them do that, John. Angel could have a genetic heart defect. Maybe Brugada Syndrome? I don't know... But I do know that if they release her tonight without more testing her heart could be a ticking time bomb in her chest."

John ran a hand through his hair. "I know. But

without a full family medical history they're not going to admit her to the hospital for testing. Especially not without health insurance."

"I'm going to talk to the attending," Charlotte snapped.

John caught her arm at the wrist before she could stalk down the hall.

"Hey." John pinched the bridge of his nose. "I think it might be time for me to take over Angel's care again."

"What are you talking about?"

John slipped his hands into his leather jacket. "I feel that I've been losing sight of some of my priorities, you know? That I might be getting out of touch with the teens. Your house will be done in the next few weeks. Who knows what's next for you?"

Charlotte's brow furrowed in frustration. "I haven't signed my contract."

"I know. But you could if you wanted to. You can go anywhere you want, Charlotte, or you can stay right here. I don't have those choices. I've got people who count on me to be there for them, and lately—like tonight—I've been letting them down."

Charlotte felt a familiar heat creeping up the back of her neck, and that prickly, itchy sensation following close behind.

"Having you here these past few months has

been…" John stopped to cough, his voice breaking. "Amazing. Charlotte, I can't thank you enough for all you've done for Piper, Angel, the teens…and me."

Charlotte wanted to press her hands to her ears.

Please stop talking…please stop talking… please stop talking.

"I don't ever want my life to be the way it was before, Charlotte. Falling in love with you has made me realize that I deserve more. The trouble is, I don't know how to get what I most want— you—without hurting someone. Like I did tonight."

Toughen up, Owens. This isn't your first rodeo. Yes, he said he loved you, but now he's changed his mind. So what? It's not like you haven't been here before. If your own father didn't want to claim you, why would John or anyone else?

"Now that Piper's leg is healed, she and I can move back onto *The House Call* tomorrow. It will make it easier for me to get the work done on it so I can list it for sale and buy a proper home."

That bitter voice was back in her head.

I told you so. I told you so. I told you so.

Then suddenly he was in front of her, cupping her face between his hands, right there, where everyone could see them.

"Charlotte, listen to me. This isn't goodbye. I just need a little time to straighten things out."

She took his hands from her face, put them back at his sides. "It's all right, John. I understand just fine. Take all the time you need. I'll wrap things up at the clinic this week and let the cruise ship know that I've completed my assignment."

"Wait… You're leaving?"

"Yes—that's generally what people do when they're no longer needed."

"I never said that."

"You don't have to say the words out loud, John. It's written all over your face. You might love me, but you're never going to trust me. Not with the hard stuff. Not with the people who matter to you. You want to save the world all alone, like some kind of superhero. But I never wanted a superhero, John. I just wanted you."

She gathered her purse and coat, eager to escape with her dignity intact. She did not want to weep in front of John or any of the hospital staff. That would have to wait until later, when she was far away from here and could put all this behind her.

John stopped her before she could storm down the hall. "Maybe you didn't want a superhero, Charlotte, but did you really want me? Imperfect, fallible, sometimes not sure what's the right thing to do? Because you sure seem willing to bolt as soon as things are less than perfect."

Charlotte looked down at his hand on her arm.

"Well, I guess we've both had a chance to speak our mind. I'm going to go see Angel now. Even if she isn't my patient anymore, I still care what happens to her."

"Charlotte!" John protested.

But then the attending appeared at John's elbow, ready to discuss Angel's case.

John looked helplessly back and forth between the attending and Charlotte. "Just…wait for me, okay?" he said.

He followed the attending out of the waiting room, all of his attention concentrated on being briefed about Angel's progress.

Charlotte watched him leave, her heart breaking into a million tiny pieces.

She made it past the reception desk and the triage area before the tears she'd held back spilled down her cheeks. She needed a few minutes to pull herself together before she saw Angel.

She paused in the hallway outside the treatment bays, leaning against the wall, her jacket folded over her arms. A nurse passed by and gave her a compassionate smile and squeezed her arm. She probably thought Charlotte had just received some terrible news about a family member. And that wasn't too far from the truth. Because what she'd had with John and Piper over the past few months had been the closest thing to family she'd had since her mother died.

"Dammit," she said, searching her bag for a clean tissue.

How many times would she have to learn the same painful lesson over and over again? Love didn't stay—at least not for her. Her fate lay in pursuing adventure, not sticking around and waiting to be rejected. She'd *known* this when she'd come here, yet she'd insisted on taking a chance.

Charlotte checked her appearance in the glass window of a treatment room. Her nose was red and her skin a bit blotchy, so she dusted some powder over her face and fluffed her hair until she felt presentable. Then she searched the emergency department until she found Angel's room. She looked tiny and wan on the hospital gurney, her face the same pale shade as the white blanket draped over her thin frame.

"Hey, Angel," Charlotte said, sitting at the end of her bed. "How are you feeling?"

Angel took a deep sip of the soda that a nurse must have given her. "Mostly good," she said, her voice lacking its usual bravado. "Maybe a little dizzy. And I have a headache."

Definitely symptoms of Brugada Syndrome, the genetic heart defect that Charlotte had feared Angel might have. But the only way to know for sure was to have Angel admitted to the hospital for extensive testing.

"The doctor said I could go home tonight. That's good, right?"

Charlotte tilted her head with a soft smile. "Usually that would be great news, Angel. But in your case that's not what I want for you."

Charlotte explained the medical condition that might be causing Angel's symptoms.

"But the only way we can get these tests done is if you let us know who you are. Then we can get a full medical history. That is, if you're okay with us talking to your family?"

Angel's expression darkened. "I don't want to be a burden to them."

"Why would helping you be a burden to your family?"

Angel looked away, out the window, her hands moving restlessly over the blankets that covered her legs. "I have three sisters, and my mom was having a hard time taking care of all of us. I thought it would be easier if I left. I'm almost fifteen now...old enough to get a job, take care of myself. It's one less mouth for my mom to feed, right?"

"Does she know where you are?"

Angel's jaw quivered. "No. I don't want her to worry. I can take care of myself now."

"Based on what you've told me so far, Angel, I'm pretty sure she wants to hear from you. And I'm certain she would want you to get help with these heart problems you're having." Charlotte pulled a pad of paper from her purse, and a pen, putting them in front of Angel. "I don't know exactly why you don't want anyone to know your real name, but I know the power that comes with seizing control of something when your world feels like it's spinning out of control. Not showing your true self does protect you from being hurt again. But it also makes you invisible. And invisible people can't be loved, because no one knows who they really are."

Angel met her gaze now, and Charlotte felt like there was a flicker of understanding in her eyes.

"Let me help you, Angel. Me and Dr. J and all the doctors here. We all want you to be safe and healthy."

Angel took a deep breath, then picked up the pen and began writing, the pen's nib making scratching sounds against the paper. Then she handed it to Charlotte.

Charlotte read the paper and smiled. "It's nice to finally meet you, Kaitlyn Webb."

A few hours later, John left the emergency room feeling like a bus had run over him slowly and repeatedly. It had been a long, grueling night of trying to convince the attending that Angel's case was more serious than simple fainting.

It was only because Charlotte had got Angel's

real name that he'd been able to call her mother and get a full medical history. Learning that her father had died in his forties of a heart attack had been enough for the attending to order more testing. Thankfully Angel would spend the next few nights in the hospital, where she would be safe and sound.

He had immediately looked for Charlotte, to share the good news, but she'd been nowhere to be found in the hospital. She hadn't responded to his texts or calls either. His last hope had been to find her car next to his at the hospital, where they had hurriedly parked when they'd come back from the marina.

But her car wasn't there.

He felt his blood run very cold. Memories of their fight about Angel's care had haunted him all night. Had he really needed to make his stand so soon after learning the news of Angel's collapse? He'd been shaken and worried, not in the best frame of mind to tell the woman he loved that he needed a little time and space to straighten out his life.

But he did. He had been living in a strange limbo for years now, and he'd never seen it until he'd fallen in love with Charlotte. Only then had he seen how his old, limiting beliefs were holding him back from living the full life he deserved. So long as he felt it was up to him and him alone to care for the teens and for Piper, he'd never be able to make room in his life for anything more interesting than a houseplant.

He checked his phone again—still no response to his texts. This was unlike Charlotte, who was as obsessive about returning calls and texts as he was. He started his car and headed for her house. Suddenly it felt very urgent that he find Charlotte right away.

Charlotte's car was in the garage. That was a good sign. But he felt very uneasy at finding her in her bedroom, with a suitcase on the bed.

"How's Angel?" she asked. But she remained where she was, her back to him as she gazed out the window.

Something wasn't right.

He moved slowly, assessing the situation. "She has an excellent prognosis, thanks to you getting her real name." His eyes roamed the room, saw the empty hangers in the closet and the counters cleared of perfume and makeup. "What's going on, Charlotte?"

She turned to him, her eyes red and puffy. "I have to go, John."

He took it all in. This seemed like an awfully strong reaction to him asking for a little space to get his life straightened out.

"I thought your assignment with *The Eden* didn't start until next month."

She sniffed and turned away. "I never signed the contract."

"So, where will you go?"

"I don't really know."

John had a well-honed radar after years of working with teens who were too young or too traumatized to verbalize their needs. He was good at reading between the lines…hearing the truth in what wasn't spoken aloud.

All this time he had believed Charlotte was someone with wanderlust in her soul—*GypsyMD*, keeping life casual and fun. But now he thought she might be something different.

"A little Greyhound therapy, then?"

She sniffed again. "What?"

"Greyhound therapy. That's what we call it at the clinic. Some of our kids think if they pack up their stuff and jump on a Greyhound bus they can leave all their problems behind. Start fresh somewhere else."

"I don't think that."

"No? Then what's happening here?"

She sat on the bed, her fingers curling round the mattress edge. When she spoke, her words were too soft for him to understand.

He took a step forward, straining to understand. "I'm sorry… You don't know how to… what?"

"I don't know how to *stay*!" she exploded, and the tears started again.

She resumed packing, channeling her nervous energy into cramming sweaters into her large suitcase. "I'm just not built like you, John. If I stay in one place for too long I start to get nervous and jumpy. Like I'm a fish in a blender... just waiting for fate to push the button. I love you, and Piper, and the teens—and even that crazy Cat who won't go away. But I'm not sure that's enough."

None of that made sense. They had worked together for months and she'd seemed perfectly comfortable at the clinic and at her house. The big change had come tonight, when he'd asked for space to straighten out some of the messes in his life. Which made sense, considering she had been doubly traumatized at a young age. First, by losing her mother to a car accident and then by her father's rejection.

What better way to make sure she was never abandoned again than to refuse to stay? Charlotte didn't travel because she had wanderlust in her soul. She traveled to avoid the connections that would break her heart if she lost them.

Every cell in his body wanted him to gather her into his arms and promise her that she was safe. That he wasn't going anywhere, and she could stop running now.

But he doubted she would listen. Not when she was this upset.

John considered his options, then headed over to the chair she had in her bedroom. He pulled it away from the wall, sat down and stretched his legs out. He opened his phone and navigated to the apps. Soon the room was full of the sound of bells and dings and whistles.

Charlotte stopped packing and looked at him. "What are you doing?"

"Some fruit-matching game that Piper taught me."

"What?"

The sounds of several bells chiming at once filled the room. "See, I just matched five lemons there—so now I have five hundred points."

Charlotte stood across from him, her arms full of sweaters. The expression on her face was pure confusion.

"Just something to do. You know... While I wait."

"Wait for what?"

He laughed. "For you, of course. Oh, wait—I need this pineapple." He made a few finger-swipes and then there were more bells and whistles. "See, the way I figure it, you can go as far away as you want. Travel all seven oceans... cross the continents. Hell, you can go to the moon. But when you've gotten all that out of your system you *will* come back to me. Because there is nothing in this universe that is stronger than the love we made the night of the hospital gala. Nothing, not even your fear, can overpower that. So do what you must. I'll be right here waiting for you. For as long as it takes."

For several long minutes Charlotte stood staring at him in disbelief. John willed himself to focus on the stupid game. Whether she left or stayed—that was up to her. But he wasn't lying. He really would wait for her. Even if he was an old man when her stubborn heart finally accepted what he already knew was true.

There was no other woman on this earth for him but her.

After a very long, uncomfortable silence, she set the sweaters down. Not in the suitcase, he noticed, which seemed like a good sign.

She finally looked at him. She looked exhausted and a little fragile.

He dropped the phone and went to her, gathered her in his arms, ready to buttress her against all the hurts of her past. She lifted her head and waited. He bent his head to kiss her, long and slow. He wanted to soothe her pain away, calm her stormy emotions and welcome her home.

But there was a strange and bitter taste in this kiss.

He searched for the sweetness he always

found in her, but found only sadness, longing, and goodbye.

Disbelief churned in his gut, making him feel sick and sad. He wanted to shake her and beg her to stay. She didn't have to go, no matter how many times she told herself she did. She could stay if she wanted. Didn't she know that? She could break the rules that were holding her hostage.

He pulled away and searched her face. That was when he knew he wasn't going to win this fight. Her mind had been made up ever since she'd left the hospital...maybe ever since she'd arrived in Seattle.

She stepped away. Touching her fingers to her mouth. Pressing her lips as if imprinting their last sad kiss there. Then she turned back to her suitcase, pushed the sweaters down, and zipped the mammoth case shut.

Every cell in his body wanted him to fight for her. But that would mean fighting *against* her, because the enemy he wanted to defeat was buried deep in her heart.

Just stay! he wanted to scream. *That's all you have to do...just stay!*

She wrestled the suitcase off the bed.

This was happening whether he liked it or not.

He sat helpless and stunned as she escaped the room and his life. There wasn't a thing he could do to change her mind. He knew better than to even try.

All he could do was wait. And hope that the trade winds would soon blow her back to him.

CHAPTER THIRTEEN

CHARLOTTE TOOK A break from eating to stretch. Her body was so achy these days. She often wondered if she was coming down with a cold, but the sniffles never came. She was probably just tired from the last few weeks.

It had been a whirlwind of goodbyes as she'd ended her assignment at The Sunshine Clinic and put her father's house on the market. She had opted to stay at a hotel until John moved out of the house and into a cute little brick house near the hospital, with plenty of room for Piper and Cat.

Charlotte had seen Angel—now Kaitlyn—one last time before she'd left for *The Eden*. Angel had come by with many of The Sunshine Clinic's regular patients to say goodbye to her. She'd had her aunt with her, with whom she was now living, and was sporting a new pacemaker that protected her heart from going into cardiac arrest. Testing had revealed she did indeed have Brugada Syndrome, and it was probably the reason her father had died so young.

But all that was behind her now. *GypsyMD* was back! Traveling the Caribbean on an unbelievably swanky cruise ship that provided every luxury and amenity she could imagine.

She looked at the dinner her medical assistant had brought. Caesar salad and roasted chicken with a few petits fours for dessert. All perfectly prepared by an award-winning chef.

But absolutely nothing looked appetizing.

"You need to eat something," her assistant had urged.

Charlotte knew she was right. She had lost ten pounds since leaving Seattle and judging from the total loss of her appetite she might lose ten more. Now her cute summer dresses just hung on her frame, when she bothered to put them on at all. All she really wanted to wear was her gray sweatpants and an old band tee shirt she'd found at the thrift store.

All this because she had tried giving up her nomadic ways to give love a chance and it had failed spectacularly.

When she had accepted the cruise ship assignment, she had planned to lose herself in everything the Caribbean cruise had to offer. Surely a few days of sea mist and warm sun would restore her soul? Then she would be ready to take advantage of the many port excursions and tours that were part of cruise life. She just had to pick which ones.

She pushed her untouched dinner away and thumbed through the brochures listlessly. Cave tubing. A historical Mayan ruin site tour. Barrier reef snorkeling. A jungle Jeep tour.

She didn't know what was wrong with her. By now her notebook should be full of ideas and itineraries, all arranged in priority order because there was never enough time to do everything she wanted. But her notebook remained blank. All she could think about was how much Piper would love cave tubing if she were here. Or how John would make his corny jokes during the Mayan ruin site tour to keep things lively.

Nothing sounded good unless she could share it with her people.

She shook off the thought. She didn't have people anymore, but what she did have was a tidy sum of money from the sale of her father's home. The money was sitting in her account, waiting to be donated to a worthy charity. She opened a new page in her notebook and wrote *Charity* across the top. If she figured out where to donate the money, maybe that would clear her head to focus on her next adventure.

There was a knock at the door. Her medical assistant said, "Dr. Owens, we have a patient complaining of chest pain."

That wasn't good. So far Charlotte's work on *The Eden* had been fairly uneventful. Plenty of sunburn cases, indigestion, and a few folks who had forgotten to pack their medicines. Nothing truly serious had happened while she was onboard, and she was hoping to keep it that way.

"Okay, please put them in Exam Room One."

"I did that. But just so you know, she's brought her husband and family with her."

"Good. I'm glad she has support." Charlotte closed up her notebook and draped her stethoscope around her neck.

"Her *very large* family," the medical assistant said with a wink.

Sure enough, the hallway outside the exam room was packed with family members of every age. The youngest was a baby, who had fallen asleep on her mother's shoulder. Everyone was wearing Hawaiian-themed shirts—which would have been a festive sight if it hadn't been for the worry on their faces.

"Excuse me," Charlotte said repeatedly as she pushed through the small crowd.

She finally made it into the exam room where an older lady was lying on the bed, her eyes closed, holding hands with a gentleman who looked to be around her age and very worried.

"Mrs. Patterson?" Charlotte said, recognizing the elderly woman who had shared her table at the hospital's fundraising gala.

The man at her side gave her shoulder a gentle shake. She opened her eyes and said, a little too loud, "What?"

The man gestured to her ear, then made a hand sign as if turning a dial up.

"Oh!" the woman said, before reaching behind her ear. Lily could see the half-moon shape of a hearing aid perched on her ear and knew Mrs. Patterson was adjusting the volume.

"The doctor's here," the man said, before taking her hand in his.

he woman squinted her eyes before she smiled in recognition. "Ah, the newlywed lady doctor. How's your husband?"

Charlotte's heart squeezed hard with a fresh wave of pain. Just seeing Mrs. Patterson brought back a flood of memories of that night with John...especially the way they'd danced together in the ballroom, and how they'd spent their time later, in his room.

Charlotte just smiled to hide her distress. She didn't want to spend time explaining her situation. Especially when Mrs. Patterson was complaining of chest pain.

"I think what's important here is you, Mrs. Patterson."

Her husband had both of his hands clasped around hers. "She started complaining of chest pain about an hour ago. We had such a lovely dinner, and then we did some dancing."

"A lot of dancing!" Mrs. Patterson laughed.

"We're celebrating our fiftieth anniversary," Mr. Patterson explained. "Our family planned this cruise as a kind of family reunion and wedding anniversary celebration."

"How lovely," Charlotte said. "I'm sure you don't want to spend your anniversary down here in the medical clinic, so let's get you checked out and on your way, shall we?"

Mrs. Patterson's vital signs were all quite stable, which made Charlotte feel a lot better. If Mrs. Patterson was having a heart attack she would likely have an irregular heartbeat, clammy skin, or shortness of breath. Still, heart attacks could be sneaky, with no warning signs, so she'd need to do an EKG to monitor Mrs. Patterson's heart activity.

The cruise ship's medical clinic had a portable EKG monitoring system that was easy and compact to use. Recordings were stored on the cloud, so if it was necessary to arrange a helicopter evacuation to a land-based hospital, a patient's test results could easily be accessed by the hospital's emergency room. This was the kind of technology that Charlotte had wanted to add to

The Sunshine Clinic. But it was expensive, and few teens needed an EKG on a regular basis, so hospital funding would never include these types of extra services.

"So, tell me how you two lovebirds met," Charlotte said as she set up the electrodes that would monitor Mrs. Patterson's heart.

She would need to be monitored for at least an hour, so Charlotte wanted to keep her mind busy and distracted from the testing at hand.

"Well, we very nearly didn't!" said Mr. Patterson, giving his wife a sweet smile. "Thanks to my wife's stubborn streak."

Mrs. Patterson laughed and waved him off. "Heavens, am I ever going to live that down?"

Charlotte pulled up a chair and made herself comfortable. "You'd better tell me the story now. You've piqued my curiosity!"

"It was all my fault," Mrs. Patterson said, folding her hands across her chest. "I went to a Halloween party with some friends in high school. When I walked in the door there was the most handsome cowboy I'd ever seen, dancing his heart out in the living room. My own heart quite literally skipped a beat when he looked my way. But he was dancing with two witches at the same time. Beautiful girls, hanging on his every word, and I decided right then and there that he must be some kind of heartbreaker who collected girl-friends like trophies."

"So when I asked this beautiful lass out on a date the next weekend she roundly turned me down," Mr. Patterson said. "And the next time and the next time and the time after that. It was embarrassing!"

Mrs. Patterson fixed her pale blue eyes on Charlotte's. "I was certain that he was only pursuing me for the challenge of it. That as soon as I said yes he'd pull his love-'em-and-leave-'em routine on me too. A routine I hadn't actually seen, by the way, but was sure he was guilty of." She patted her husband's hand affectionately. "As it turned out the two beautiful ladies he was dancing with were his cousins, visiting from out of town for a long weekend."

"I've never collected girlfriends!" Mr. Patterson said indignantly. "I've got my hands full with this one!"

The long-married couple gazed at each other as if they'd just met a few hours earlier. Charlotte smiled at their obvious love for each other.

"And to think," Mrs. Patterson said, "if I hadn't ever learned the truth about you, none of this would have happened!" She waved her hand to indicate the family members who were standing around or sitting on the floor, waiting for news of her health.

An hour later, Charlotte removed the electrodes and gave the Mrs. Patterson the good news that her heart was strong and healthy. "You may have just overdone it with the anniversary celebrations," she told her. "Take it easy for the next few days, don't hit the all-you-can-eat buffet too hard, and come back to see me if anything seems amiss."

The Pattersons and their multi-generational family left the clinic in much better spirits than when they'd entered. And Charlotte's heart felt lighter too, now she knew the couple would be able to enjoy their anniversary trip and hopefully many more years together.

Charlotte closed up the clinic and headed back to her cabin. Her mind was full of the story that Mrs. Patterson had shared. Especially how the Pattersons' love story would never have happened if she hadn't learned the truth about her hopeful suitor.

Then she thought of Angel—Kaitlyn—and how she'd risked her health because she'd thought she was a burden to her family.

And Piper, who'd assumed that getting herself into trouble at school would get her reunited with her father.

And John, who'd thought asking for help for the clinic would be a sign of weakness, when in fact the Seattle community very much wanted to take care of its at-risk teens.

How many self-destructive things do we do when we don't know the truth? Charlotte wondered.

Which made it impossible to avoid thinking about her own decisions—especially the ones that had led her here.

"This isn't goodbye, Charlotte. I just need a little time..."

John had straight out told her what he needed. But all she'd heard were echoes of her father's rejection and abandonment. She hadn't been able to get past her own fears and really listen to what John needed. So she had made decisions for him, for both of them, that were really just about protecting her ego.

It's too late. He wouldn't want to see me now after what I did to us.

And there they were again. Her assumptions and beliefs about what John would do, without ever giving him a chance to speak for himself.

The truth was, she didn't know what he would say. Maybe she was right. Maybe he never wanted to see her again.

It would break her heart if that were true, but she still had to try.

She had to be stronger than her fears if she ever hoped to have a real life for herself. A life that looked like the Pattersons', full of love and a devotion so strong that it created two more generations.

But before she went back to Seattle there was one more truth she needed to face. One more person she had not allowed to have his say.

Charlotte closed the door to her cabin and went to the closet. She had packed up in a hurry once her father's house had sold, so she wasn't sure what documents had come with her and which ones were packed away in storage. She flipped past her medical license, the house sale contract, her employment contract with *The Eden*. Towards the back, she finally found what she was looking for.

She held the envelope, its ivory paper thick and expensive, for several long minutes. She ran her finger across her name, *Dr. Charlotte Owens*, written in her father's script across the front. It felt like her entire life had come down to this one letter.

She took a deep breath and flipped it over, running her finger under the seal to break it.

The new built-in desk was an excellent addition to the office, giving John and the clinic's second doctor a dedicated space for their computer and files. Much classier than the old door he'd lain across two sawhorses.

He wished Charlotte were here to see it.

The very thought of her was enough to form a thick lump in his throat. His body still felt utterly exhausted from the hard work of grieving over their breakup.

He'd kept hoping she'd come back, or call, or in some way reach out to him…give them a second chance. But she was gone in every sense of the word.

She hadn't even updated her travel blog, which had worried him at first. But the hospital had assured him that they had spoken to her when she'd ended her assignment, so he knew she was okay. She just didn't want to speak to him.

Sarah poked her head into John's office. "Don't forget that meeting with the chief at two o'clock this afternoon!"

"I won't," John assured her. "Now go on with yourself. There's a retirement with your name written all over it."

He got up to walk her to the door, knowing that otherwise Sarah would find a hundred more little tasks she needed to do before she officially retired.

"Oh, John…" Sarah lamented. "I can't imagine not seeing you and the kids every day. Are you sure you're going to be all right?"

John stooped to give her a kiss. "I'll be fine, Sarah, though I'm sure going to miss you. Without you, I don't think The Sunshine Clinic would ever have happened."

Sarah reached out to give John one of her signature bear hugs, and he gratefully accepted.

"You would have found a way, John. You always do."

John walked Sarah to her car and wished her well. He had a new medical assistant now, and a new receptionist to replace Sarah now she'd announced she was finally ready to retire. She meant it this time.

There had been other changes to the clinic too. Like the breathing treatment area that Charlotte had suggested, and a steady stream of nursing students who worked every afternoon to earn practicum hours toward their degrees and provided John with free staffing. There was a nutritionist who came every Friday afternoon, and there were plans to add a dentist and a hygienist two or three days a week.

But the best thing of all was the ten-year plan that the hospital had developed for The Sunshine Clinic, with John's input taking priority. In due time, the clinic would move into a bigger building that could accommodate more doctors, nurses, and other specialists, who would provide all the services John had always dreamed of.

It was like a dream come true, and it had all

started the night he'd given his speech from the heart at the fundraising gala.

As it turned out there were a lot of doctors and administrators who wanted to help Seattle's disadvantaged teens. They just hadn't known that John needed more donations, more volunteers, and a bigger budget—because he had never asked. Now that the hospital's board of directors were aware of his ambitions and needs, a lot more funding and support had been sent his way.

Which was why he had a monthly meeting with the chief of pediatrics to discuss the clinic's progress and growth. But the chief's emails had been rather cryptic of late, hinting at some new initiative the hospital had in mind for the clinic. Despite his best efforts, John hadn't been able to get his boss or any of his colleagues to spill any beans about this new plan.

John gathered his files and notes for the meeting. Then paused in the hallway outside the door he still thought of as Charlotte's office. But Charlotte wasn't there anymore, and she wasn't coming back. He had a new part-time pediatrician now, who worked a few afternoons a week, and on-call doctors filling in the rest of the time. It was more help than he'd had since he started the clinic, but it wasn't Charlotte…

John usually made good use of his driving time by listening to pediatric medicine podcasts, so he could keep up with the latest research and treatment options. But he just wasn't in the mood today, so he searched the radio until he found a smooth jazz station. It reminded him of the night he had driven Charlotte home from the clinic after their street call work. It had felt so good to take care of her when she was so exhausted after Tommy's close call with death.

But it didn't feel good to remember their fight at the hospital when Angel had collapsed.

"You might love me, but you're never going to trust me...not with the people who matter to you."

A superhero. That was what she'd called him. She'd said that he just wanted to save the world alone, like some kind of superhero.

That was crazy, he'd thought when she'd first left. The last thing in the world he felt like was a superhero of any kind. Superheroes didn't have brothers who fell apart right in front of them, or nieces who wanted to fight their way into jail.

But that had been a few months ago, and he saw things differently now. Especially now he knew how much his colleagues wanted to help the clinic once he had told them the truth during his speech at the gala. He really couldn't do everything he wanted for the teens all by himself.

So, Charlotte was right.

He had fallen head over heels in love with her. But he hadn't been willing to fully trust her with all of his vulnerabilities. To let her know that he needed her at the clinic and in his life.

John pulled into one of the parking spaces at the hospital for medical staff and made his way to his boss's office. Her assistant directed him to the conference room and offered him a coffee while he waited.

"She'll just be a few moments. She's invited a guest to join you today. Someone who is familiar with the new community initiative the hospital wants to explore."

It was really driving John crazy that no one would tell him what was going on. It had been like this for weeks—ever since the hospital had gained a new donor who was apparently putting some stipulations on their donation. John hoped it wasn't going to become a problem.

Eventually John had waited long enough to need a refill on his coffee. He was doctoring his coffee with two creams and sugar when he heard the conference room door open.

"Hey, Dr. Fagan," John said, without looking up. "Can I get you a coffee?"

"Sure. Two creams, please. But I guess you already know that."

John's world froze as he recognized her voice. He slowly turned and faced her. She was even more beautiful than he remembered, her long hair falling in waves around her face and her skin now tanned from the time she had spent in the Caribbean.

"What are you doing here?" he managed to say, amazed that his brain was still able to form words.

"I have something to show you," she said, tucking her hair behind her ear.

"I can't go anywhere right now. I'm about to have a meeting with the chief of pediatrics and a new donor to the clinic."

She smiled and, damn, if his heart didn't skip a beat. "I believe I *am* that donor, John. And I'd like to show you what I've donated."

This entire situation had rendered John mute, and he had no choice but to follow her like an obedient puppy. She led him out of the conference room to the elevators outside the chief's office. It was too soon and too awkward for any kind of conversation, so he simply stood in silence next to her, smelling that jasmine-scented perfume she favored, which stirred memories of their last elevator ride together.

Those memories were too provocative, so he forced himself to concentrate on the ever-decreasing floor numbers as they descended to the parking garage.

"Where are we going?" he asked, as she walked him out of the garage toward a fenced lot next to the hospital. This was where the hospital's ambulances parked when they were off duty.

"This way," she said.

When they rounded the corner, John was shocked to discover the chief of pediatrics was there, along with other colleagues from the pediatrics department. And Sarah too.

They were all flanking a large blue vehicle that John had never seen before, but which bore the name of his clinic. Only it said *The Sunshine Mobile Clinic for Kids*.

John looked to Charlotte. "I don't understand..."

Dr. Fagan appeared at his side, all smiles and handshakes. "Congratulations, John. You're the proud owner of a new forty-foot mobile health clinic, equipped with two exam rooms, an onboard laboratory, and telehealth equipment so your patients can access specialists all over North America. All thanks to the extremely generous donation of your former locum tenens Dr. Owens. I've been trying to woo her to come back and work for us full-time, but she's playing hard to get. Maybe you'll have better luck."

With that, Dr. Fagan opened the door to the mobile clinic so that the pediatric team could get their first tour, leaving John and Charlotte alone.

John searched for the right words. "This is amazing, Charlotte. Thank you so much. But I don't understand..."

"It was my father's letter, I guess."

"You read it, then?"

"Yes, and now I want to read it to you."

She led John by the hand to a picnic table under some trees and sat across from him. She pulled a letter from her purse, then smoothed the paper with her hands. Her voice was shaky but clear as she read to him the words she had avoided for so long.

Dear Charlotte,

Words cannot express my regret at having to write this letter. If I had lived my life properly, a letter such as this would never be necessary. Unfortunately, I made choices I deeply regret. And, while I can never take back the harm I have caused you, I can at least give you a full accounting of the details.

I met your beautiful mother the summer before I went to college. I was bright and energetic, destined to attend a good college and become a good attorney, like my father and his father before that. Your mother waited tables at a café my friends and I liked to visit, and I thought she was just about the most amazing creature I had ever seen. What started as a harmless flirtation blossomed into a full-blown love af-

fair. She was all I could think about every minute of every day.

A few weeks before I was scheduled to leave for college, we discovered your mother was pregnant. And while I was thrilled, and confident we'd find a way to raise you while finishing our educations, my parents had a very different reaction. They gave me an ultimatum—I could choose you and your mother and forfeit the family trust fund that would pay for my college. Or I could walk away from both of you and everything would be as if it had never happened.

I think my choice is obvious, and I will never be able to make up for the hard years you and your mother endured. There is no excuse for what I did. I was young and afraid and convinced I couldn't survive without my family's support.

Years later, when your mother died, I forfeited my parental rights rather than face you. I couldn't imagine that you wouldn't hate me for my choices. I foolishly assumed that you would be placed with a relative on your mother's side. That was not the case, as I learned much later, when making plans for my estate.

In the end, Charlotte, all of my choices were for naught. The legal career I valued

above you failed me when my business part-
ner embezzled funds, leaving our firm des-
titute and in legal jeopardy. Everything I
worked for slipped through my fingers like
sand. And why shouldn't it? A house that's
built on a shaky foundation is destined to
fall in times of trouble.

Now, at the end of my life, all I have left
in the world is this house, and it's in about
as good of shape as I am. I hope in some
small way it will bring good to your life.
And I hope that you'll be smarter than I was.

Charlotte, when something—or someone—
good comes your way, you grab on tight and
don't ever let it go.

Charlotte folded the letter into thirds and
slipped it back into its envelope. John noticed
how worn the paper was and suspected that she
had read and reread the letter many times.

"It was Mrs. Patterson who inspired me to read
the letter. You remember her from the gala, right?
She was on a cruise with her family on *The Eden*
and had a bit of a health scare. She was fine,
thank goodness, but talking to her and her husband and meeting her family made a bit of an
impression on me."

Charlotte paused to tuck some errant strands

of hair behind her ear. She seemed different now, he noticed. More confident than he remembered.

Despite their many months apart, John had the strongest urge to pull her into his arms, tuck her against his chest. He knew how hard that must have been for her, reading a letter from the man who was responsible for the hardest years of her life. But she wasn't his to comfort anymore, so he willed his hands to remain at his sides while she spoke.

"I'm afraid I'm guilty of making the same mistakes as my father," Charlotte said, her blue eyes dark and solemn. "I fell in love with you and Piper and The Sunshine Clinic. I knew you were my home, John, and that I belonged here. But at the first sign of trouble I dived back into the life I knew instead of doing what was right. I should have been there for you after Angel's collapse, even if you needed some space to deal with your emotions. Instead, I balked and bolted, so I didn't have to risk you rejecting me."

"I was never going to abandon you, Charlotte. I just didn't know how to love you without someone getting hurt or overlooked."

She reached out for his hand. "I know that now. Which is why I wanted to donate the proceeds of my father's house sale to The Sunshine Clinic. Now you can bring those corny jokes to even more at-risk teens in Seattle, whether they want to hear them or not."

He pulled her to him now, close enough that he could see the dark circles of her pupils and the lush, full lips that he longed to kiss. "I don't suppose I could interest you in an exciting travel assignment on the streets of Seattle?"

She tilted her head up in an unmistakable invitation to pick up where they had left off. "I don't suppose you could keep me away, Dr. Bennett."

Finally, she was his. Really, truly his. And it seemed like the heavens should open so that legions of angels could tumble from the sky and serenade them where they stood. But that didn't happen, so he settled for a long, sweet, slow kiss that would start the next chapter of their lives.

EPILOGUE

One year later

CHARLOTTE HAD JUST smashed a perfectly good bottle of champagne.

It was a beautiful Saturday in June, and John and Charlotte had invited all their friends, who were really their family, to join them for an official christening ceremony for their new sailboat, *Two Docks and a Boat*.

Piper was hosting her first playdate on their new, larger sailboat. She practically beamed as she showed her friend how to dock and tie off the boat, along with all the other boating chores she'd learned since living with John.

Piper's friendships were blossoming at school, and playdates like these were becoming a regular occurrence in her life. She and John were visiting Michael regularly now and had invited Charlotte to join them for their next visit. Charlotte was looking forward to meeting her future brother-in-law, and eventually helping him start his life over with her and John for support.

John was busy on the deck of their new boat, cooking burgers for a summer picnic. Charlotte went up behind him and gave him a hug. "Look what we've done here," she said.

John paused in his work and watched the party unfold. The air was filled with the chatter of excited teens, many from the clinic, catching up with Angel/Kaitlyn and her new life.

Seagulls circled overhead, hoping for their chance at a stolen hamburger bun, while the sun shone over it all.

"We made this," Charlotte said, her heart full to bursting. "Our own little family."

John slipped an arm around her and grazed his lips against hers. "You think you'll miss jungle tours in the Caribbean? Or snow-skiing in Vail?"

Charlotte chuckled. "Definitely!" She looked down at the hand that John had splayed protectively against her belly. "But I think our little guy will provide enough adventure for me for quite some time."

John nuzzled her ear. "Should we tell everyone now or later?"

She leaned back against him, loving the solid strength of him. "Later, I think."

For now, she wanted to bask in the quiet refuge of his arms, safe in the knowledge that she had found her way home.

* * * * *